The
Consul's File

The Consul's File

PAUL THEROUX

HOUGHTON MIFFLIN COMPANY BOSTON

1977

Some of these stories first appeared in *The Atlantic, Confrontation, Encounter, Harpers and Queen, The London Magazine, New Statesman, North American Review, Penthouse, Playboy, Redbook, The Times* (London), *The Times Anthology of Ghost Stories, The Transatlantic Review,* and *TriQuarterly.*

Library of Congress Cataloging in Publication Data

Theroux, Paul.
  The consul's file.

  I. Title.
PZ4.T394Co [PS3570.H4]   813'.5'4   77–6431
ISBN 0–395–25399–3

Printed in the United States of America

V   10   9   8   7   6   5   4   3   2   1

Contents

The
Consul's File

1. The Consul's File

IT WAS a late recessional, one of the last in Asia. The Consulate in that little town had been necessary to the American rubber estates, but the rubber trees were being replaced by oil palms, and most of the Americans had left. It was my job to phase out the Consulate. In other places the consular task was, in the State Department phrase, bridge-building; in Ayer Hitam I was dismantling a bridge — not a difficult job: we had never been very popular with the Malays.

I was unmarried; I had time on my hands. Because I had been told that everything I needed to know was in the files that were kept in the box-room of the Residence, for a long time I avoided looking through them. I had other ideas, and whether it was the annoyance of being known in that place as just another white man or the pointless pressure of the bureaucracy I served, I felt a need to stake a claim, so I might carry a bit of that town away undistorted. In a different age I might have taken a Malay mistress, but in my restless mood — excited by what I saw and yet feeling a little like a souvenir hunter — I decided to write.

The place, people said, was full of stories. One of the first ones I heard — told to me by a member of the Ayer Hitam Club (it concerned a planter on whom a Malay woman had placed a bizarre curse; the planter died of hiccups in Aden, and the man who told me the story claimed he had been in an adjoining stateroom) — I later read in a volume of Somerset Maugham in the club library.

I would write only what I knew to be true, or what I could verify. But the stories were elusive, and I sometimes wondered what another writer would make of them. For example, soon after I arrived there was a grass fire in a nearby village. In itself, this was not remarkable; but the fire had unlikely consequences. The economy of this village was based mainly on the sale of marijuana that grew in tall stalks all around it, a green weed that was made into *bhang*. It was intensively cultivated and nearly all of it was exported by smugglers. A fire had started — no one knew how — and it burned for days, first in the dry brush that lay under the marijuana, and finally consuming the marijuana itself and turning it into the bittersweet smoke of the narcotic.

The villagers were safe; their houses were surrounded by wide dirt compounds in which nothing grew. Instead of bolting when the fire started, they stayed where they were. And a strange thing happened: for five days, breathing the smoke from the grass fire, they remained high, staggering and yelling, beating gongs and behaving like madmen. They were people who had never tasted alcohol, orthodox Muslims who threw villagers in jail for eating during the daylight hours of Ramadhan. But they inhaled the smoke and forgot their prayers; they rolled in the dust, pounced on each other, ran naked through the *kampong*, and burnt a Chinese shop. Afterwards they were ashamed and stopped growing the weed, and a delegation of them made the *haj* to Mecca to ask Allah's forgiveness.

I thought it was a great story, but I could never make more of it than that. I had only the incident. "That would make a terrific story," people said at the Club. But that was the whole of it; to add more would be to distort it; it was extraordinary and so — in all senses — incidental. But stories like that convinced the club members that the town was teeming with "material."

They were an odd crowd who treasured their oddity. They thought of themselves as "characters" — this was a compliment in that place and the compliment was expected to be repaid. They verified each other's uniqueness: Angela Miller's dog had once had a hernia, Squibb had met Maugham at the Sultan's coronation, Alec Stewart often went to work in his pajamas, Strang the surveyor had grown watercress in his gumboots, Duff Gillespie had once owned a Rolls-Royce. But there is something impersonal in the celebration of eccentricity. No one mentioned that Angela had had a nervous breakdown and still, frequently, went into the billiard room to cry, that Alec was married to a Chinese girl half his age, that Squibb — who had a wife in England — was married to a very fat Malay woman, or that Strang's wife, who was pretty and rapacious, danced with every member but her husband; and when *Suzie Wong* was staged at the Club no one commented on the fact that Suzie was played not by a Chinese girl but by a middle-aged and fairly hysterical Englishwoman.

Nor did anyone find it strange that in a place where there were Hindu *bhajans*, Malay weddings and shadow plays, and Chinese operas, the club members' idea of a night out was the long drive to Singapore to see a British *Carry On* movie, which they would laugh about for weeks afterward. They remarked on the heat: it was hot every day of the year. They didn't notice the insects, how every time a mosquito was slapped it left a smear of blood in your palm; they didn't mention the white ants, which were everywhere and ate everything. Their locutions were tropical: any sickness was a fever, diarrhea was dysentery, every rainfall a monsoon. It wasn't romance, it was habit.

The town was some shops, the Club, the mission, the dispensary, the Methodist school, my consulate. The Indians lived on the rubber estates, the Malays in neighboring *kampongs*, the Chinese in their shops. The town was flat; in the dry season it was dusty, in the wet season flooded; it was always hot. It had no history that anyone could remember, although during the war the Japanese had used one of its old houses as headquarters for the attack on Singapore. The Club had once had polo-ponies and had won many matches against the Sultan; but all that remained were the trophies — the stables had been converted to staff quarters. Apart from tennis, the Club had no games, and the table in the billiard room where Angela Miller sometimes went to cry was torn and unusable.

After my first week in the town I thought I knew everything there was to know about the place; I had seen it all, I felt, and would not have minded leaving and going back to Africa where I had begun my career in the Foreign Service. The early sunlight saddened me and made me remember Africa; and yet the sun illuminated my mind as well, each dawn lending its peculiar light to my dreams. I had never dreamed much in America, but this tropical sun stirred me and I began to associate it with imagination, like the heat and noise that always woke me with a feeling of my own insignificance.

The unvarying heat, so different from the chilly weather I had known in Africa, had a curious effect on me: I had no sense of time passing — one day was just like another — and I felt puny and very old, as if my life were ending in this hot town in the East that was so small and remote it was like an island.

I had not started writing, since I considered writing my last resort. I would familiarize myself with the town by reading the files, and when I had done that and had no more excuses I would begin writing, if I still felt restless and unoccupied. I would not write much about myself; I would concentrate on the town, this island in which more and more, as they became friendly and candid, so many people said nothing ever happened.

Miss Leong, my secretary, had told me about the files. She had never seen them, but a succession of consuls had referred to them. They were secret; they were the reason my predecessors had chosen to take days off to work undisturbed at the Residence. Miss Leong was confidential, and she gave me the key, which in her loyal Chinese way she had never used. She transmitted this sense of mystery to me, of the secrets that lay in the box-room of the Residence, and it seemed to give my job an importance greater than any I could achieve as a writer of stories. Of the three men in the Foreign Service I knew to be writers, two were failures in their diplomatic duties and the third ended up selling real estate in Maryland.

I gave Ah Wing, my houseboy, the day off; I told Miss Leong that I was working at home; and I opened the box-room. It was very dusty, and when I walked in cobwebs brushed my eyes and trailed down my face. I smelled decayed wood and the peanut-stink of dead insects. The room was small and hot and just being there made me itch. I found some cardboard boxes and, inside, stacks of paper bound with string. I didn't have to untie the string: I lifted it and it broke and I saw that what it had held were ragged yellow papers in which white ants had chewed their way to nest. Many of the ants were dead, but there were still live ones hurrying out of the chewed pages. Another story, dramatic: the consuls' files made illegible by the white ants, because the files were hidden and secret. Well, that was true, but I did not have to look for long to discover that there was little writing on them, and certainly no secrets; in fact, most of the pages were blank.

2. Dependent Wife

A ROAD, some gum trees, a row of shop-houses, three parked cars: Ayer Hitam was that small, and even after we parked in front of the coffee shop I was not sure we had arrived. But apparently this was all — this and a kind of low dense foliage that gave, in the way it gripped the town, a hint of strangulation. It was to be months before I made anything of this random settlement. It seemed at times as if I was inventing the place. I could find no explanation for its name, which meant "Black Water."

The trip had started gloomy with suppressed argument. Flint, number two in the Embassy in Kuala Lumpur, had offered to drive me down and show me around. With no Malay *syce* to inhibit conversation I had expected a candid tour — Flint had been recommended to me as an old Malaysian hand. I needed information to give life to the position papers and the files of clippings I'd studied all summer in Washington. The Political Section had briefed me in K.L., but the briefing had been too short, and when finally I was alone with the Press Officer he launched into a tedious monologuing — a clinical dithyramb about his bowel movements since arriving in the country.

Flint also had other things on his mind. As soon as the road straightened he said, "The Foreign Service isn't what it was. I remember when an overseas post meant some excitement. Hard work, drinking, romance, a little bit of the Empire. I never looked for gratitude, but I felt I was doing a real job."

" 'The White Man's Burden,' " I said.

Flint said, "That's my favorite poem. Someday I'll get plastered and recite it to you. People think it's about the British in India. It isn't. It's about us in the Philippines. It's a heartbreaking poem — it makes me cry." He smacked his lips in regret. "God, I envy you. You're on your own here. The telephone will be out of order half the time, there's a decent club, and no one'll bother you. It's just the kind of job I had in Medan in sixty-two, sixty-three."

"It doesn't have much strategic value."

"Never mind that," said Flint. "It's a bachelor post."

I've always hated the presumption in that phrase; like *dirty weekend* it strikes me as only pathetic. I said, "We'll see."

"It's no reflection on you," he said. "They don't send married men to places like Ayer Hitam anymore. Sure, I'd be off like a shot, but Lois wouldn't stand for it." He was silent for a while, then he tightened his grip on the steering wheel and said, "It's in the air, this dependent wife business."

I said, "At that party in K.L. the other night I met a very attractive girl. I asked her what she did. She said, 'I'm a wife.' "

"See what I mean? I bet she was eating her heart out. Hates the place, hates her husband, bores the pants off everyone with what it means to be a woman."

"It was a silly question," I said. "She seemed happy enough."

"She's climbing the walls," said Flint. "They hate the designation — dependent wife. Lois is going crazy."

"I'm sorry to hear it."

He shrugged, bringing his shoulders almost to his ears. "I've got a job to do. She's supposed to be involved in it, but she refuses to give dinner parties."

I said, "They're a lot of work."

"The hell they are — she's got three goddamned servants!" Flint glowered at the road. For miles we had been passing rubber estates: regular rows of slender trees scored with cuts, like great wilted orchards crisscrossed by perfectly straight paths, a yellowing symmetry that made the landscape seem hot and violated. I had expected a bit more than this. "And sometimes — I'm not kidding — sometimes she refuses to go to dinner parties with me. We've got one tonight — I'll have to drag her to it." He squinted. "I *will* drag her, too. She says I'm married to my job."

"I can sympathize with some of these wives," I said. "They get married right out of college, the husband gets an overseas post and everything's fine — the woman becomes a hostess. Then she sees that what she's really doing is boosting her husband in his job. What's in it for her?"

"I'll tell you what's in it for her," said Flint, turning angry again. "She's got three square meals, duty-free booze, a beautiful home, and all the servants she wants. No dishes, no laundry, no housework. And for that we get kicked in the teeth."

"I wouldn't know about that."

"Then listen," said Flint. "Lois is upset, but the younger ones are bent out of shape. Sure, they're pleasant when you first meet them, but later on you find out they're really hostile. They want jobs, they want to read the cables, they write letters to *Stars and Stripes* and sign them 'Disgusted.' Then they corner the Ambassador's wife and start bending her ear."

"We had a few problems like that in Uganda."

"This isn't a problem, it's an international incident." Now

Flint was pounding the steering wheel as he spoke. "The wives in Saigon — you know whose side they were on? The Vietcong! I won't name names but a lot of those gals in Saigon got it into their heads that they were oppressed, and believe me they supported the V.C. No, they didn't give speeches, but they nagged and nagged. They talked about 'our struggle' as if there was some connection between the guerillas shelling Nhatrang and a lot of old hens in the embassy compound refusing to make peanut-butter sandwiches. It's not funny. I knew lots of officers who were shipped home — their wives were a security risk." Then Flint added warily, "You probably think I'm making this up. I'm not. They don't want to give dinner parties, they don't wear dresses anymore — just these dungarees and sweatshirts. They hate coffee mornings. 'What do you do?' 'I'm a wife.' Whoever said that to you — I'm not asking — is a very unhappy woman."

In this way, when he could have been filling me in on Ayer Hitam, Flint ranted for the entire trip from K.L. When we arrived at the coffee shop he was a bit breathless and disappointed, as if he wished to continue the journey to continue his rant.

The door of the car was snatched open. Outside was a woman of about thirty, not fat but full-faced, yellow-brown, with thick arms and a tremendous grin. She wore a *sarong kebaya*, and her feet, which were bare, were so dirty I took them at first for shoes. She saw the two of us and let out a cry of gratitude and joy, a kind of welcoming yelp.

It had started to rain, large widely spaced drops going *phut* at the roadside and turning to dust.

She said, "It's raining! That means good luck!" She ran around to Flint's side of the car, tugged his sleeve and dragged him to a seat on the verandah, repeating her name, which was Fadila.

"Yes, yes," she said. "Two coffees and what else? Beer? I got some cold Tiger bottles waiting for you. You want a bowl of Chinese noodles? *Nasi goreng? Laksa?* Here, have a cigarette." She offered us a round can of mentholated cigarettes and muttered for a small Chinese boy to leave us alone. "Welcome to Ayer Hitam. Relax, don't be stuffy."

We thanked her and she said something that sounded like "Hawaii." We persuaded her to say it more slowly. She said, "Have you a wife?"

"Not him," said Flint, slapping me on the arm in what I am sure he meant as congratulation.

"I'm coming," she said.

She left. Flint said, "I've never seen her before."

"Seems very friendly."

"Typical," said Flint, full of approval. "The Malays are fantastic. You get people like this all over the Federation — plenty of time for small talk, very hospitable, give you the shirt off their back. I got this theory. You ask a guy directions in Malaysia. If the guy's Chinese he knows where you want to go but he won't tell you how to get there. If he's Indian he knows and he'll tell you. If he's Malay he won't know the place but he'll talk for ten hours about everything else. It's the temperament. Friendly. No hangups. Outgoing. All the time in the world."

Fadila was back with the coffees. "Americans, right?" she said, slopping coffee into the saucers as she set down the cups. "I know Americans. Just had some here the other day, three of them, going down to Singapore. 'Why go to Singapore?' I said. 'Why not stay here?' I gave them a good meal, some free beer. Why not? I don't care if the manager gets cross. It's good for business — they'll be back. That's how you get customers." She grinned at Flint, who had been listening to this with interest. "Hey, they invited me to visit them in New York City!"

Flint said, "You wouldn't like New York."

"Why not? I like K.L. I like Johore Bahru. I like Seremban. Why not New York? What's your line of work, mister?"

Ordinarily, someone like Flint would have said "business"
or "teaching" or made some vague reference to the government service. But Fadila was friendly; Fadila had spooned
sugar into his coffee and stirred it; Fadila was snapping her
hanky at the flies near the table. So Flint was truthful: "I'm
with the U.S. Embassy in K.L. This is your new consul. Mr.
Rogers's replacement."

Fadila brightened and became even more voluble. "Any-
thing you want to know I can tell you." She winked at me.
"There's something going on here. More than you think.
You don't know, mister. I hear everything. Stay here."

This time she rushed away.

Flint said, "Jesus, I envy you. This is the real Malaysia.
Look how friendly they are!"

"They? You mean *her*."

"They're all like that in these little towns. And I'm stuck
in K.L. Maybe Lois is right — I *am* married to my job — but
if it wasn't for her I could be in a place like this. And tonight
I've got this dinner, another hassle."

Fadila hurried toward us along the verandah. She was
wearing a pair of sunglasses with one cracked lens and carrying
two pint bottles of Tiger beer. She placed them on the table
and opened them.

"It's rather early for that," I said.

"It's free," she said, snorting. "It's a present. You're my
guests. Drink it up."

Flint was smiling. He drank. I drank. The beer was sweet
and heavy, and on top of the coffee fairly nauseating. Fadila
talked as we drank; now she was saying something about the
Malays — she didn't trust them, they stole, they were lazy,

they were sneaky, they lied. She knew they lied: they were always lying about her. The British were good people, but she liked Americans best of all. I listened, but she did not require any encouragement. I concentrated on finishing the bottle of beer and when I had drunk it all I felt dazed, sickened, leaden, no longer hungry, and slightly myopic, as if the beer had been squirted in my eyes.

I said, "We have to go."

"What's the rush?" said Flint. "I'm enjoying myself."

Fadila said, "Anyway, the Residence isn't ready."

Flint looked interested.

"You have to stay at the Club — they're still painting the Residence."

Flint said, "They were supposed to have finished that painting last week."

Fadila shook her head. "I know the *jaga* — they're not finished. But the Club is nice. I'll see you there, don't worry. I know the Head Boy, Stanley Chee. Tell him Fadila sent you. He'll take good care of you."

I stood up and thanked her for the beer. Flint said, "I was just telling my friend here how lucky he is to have a post like this."

"It's quiet in Ayer Hitam," she said. "No rat-race here, like K.L. You can relax."

And in the car Flint said, "Aren't these people fantastic?"

We went to the Consulate, a three-room bungalow made into offices, flying an American flag. It faced directly onto the road, at the beginning of the long driveway which led to the Residence, where another flag flew on a taller pole. I was introduced to my secretary, Miss Leong, to the driver Abubaker, and to the *peon* Peeraswami. They looked apprehensive; they were silent, stiff with worry, seeing their new employer for the first time. I felt sorry for them and tried to relieve their anxiety by staying a while to chat, but this only worried them the more, and indeed the longer I chatted the more their terror of me seemed to increase.

Although it was only a hundred yards away, we drove to the Residence, and Flint — perhaps remembering Medan — said, "White men don't walk."

The Residence was blistered and scorched, the columns blackened, the verandah mottled; it had the appearance of having withstood a siege. But it was the workmen, burning off the old paint with blowtorches. They scurried out of broken bushes and set to work as soon as we drove in. Fadila's warning had been accurate: there was a great deal more to do. Bamboo scaffolding had been lashed together around the house, and it tottered as the workmen clung with their flames and scrapers. I could see into and through the house: it was empty but for a figure running out at the back, shooing chickens, slamming doors.

Flint said, "They should have finished this painting a week ago."

We turned to go. Fadila was leaning against the car. She was smiling, in her sunglasses, and now I could see how dirty her sarong was, the torn blouse, her grubby feet.

She said, "I knew where to find you."

Flint looked pleased, but when he started to talk to her she shouted something quickly in Malay to the painters. She laughed and said, "I told them to mind their own business and get to work. No fooling and what not. The *Tuans* are watching you. Look, they are afraid."

"Why, thanks very much," said Flint.

But I said to her, "That won't be necessary."

Flint glanced at me as if to warn me that I'd been too sharp with her.

"We've got work to do," I said.

Fadila said, "The Consulate closes for lunch." She looked at the sun out of the corner of her eye. "Almost time."

"Shall we go over to the Club?" said Flint.

"I'll show you where it is," said Fadila.

I said, "We'll find it."

"Look," she said, pointing at the painters. "Look at those stupid men. I tell them to work and they don't work. Now they are just sitting." She screamed at them in Malay and this time they replied, seeming to mock her. It was then that I noticed Fadila's very dirty hair.

Flint said, "Fadila will keep them on their toes, won't you sweetheart?"

"They are pigs," she said. "Malay people are no good." She spat in their direction. "They are dirty and lazy. They try to do things to me. Yes! But I don't let them."

"What kind of things?" asked Flint, savoring the risk in his question.

"With my head."

I said, "Let's go."

But Flint was still talking to Fadila. He said, "This is a great place. I'd like to be here myself."

"You stay here," said Fadila coyly; then she motioned to me. "He can go back to K.L."

The club dining room was full: men in sports shirts, shorts, and knee socks, women in summer dresses, waiters in stiff jackets and ties carrying trays. It was as if we had stumbled into a lost world, but not an ancient one; here it was eternally 1938. None of the people looked directly at us, and no one had greeted us, but this exaggerated lack of interest made me as uncomfortable as if we were being stared at. A silence had fallen when we entered, then the silence became a rustling of self-consciousness, the clatter of forks, laughter, and loud talking.

Flint said, "I think I've made a friend." After we ordered he said, "I need a friend."

"I'll keep an eye on her."

"You were acting pretty funny with her," he said. "They're all right, these people. We could learn a lot from them. They look after their menfolk, they know how to run a house, they got a good sense of humor. You won't hear any dependent wife crap from them."

I said nothing. I continued to eat, and I felt the attention of everyone in the room on me, the pressure of their glances; I sensed them sniffing.

Flint said, "You won't get anywhere if you take that attitude."

I looked at him, wishing he'd shut up.

He said, "That high and mighty attitude, thinking people like Fadila don't matter. They do. And I'll tell you something else — she knows a lot that goes on around here." He tapped his head. "She's tuned in."

"She could use a bath," I said.

"Uncalled-for," he said. "You don't know how lucky we've been. We arrive in town and, bingo, we meet the greatest character in the place. I'll bet everyone knows her."

He could not have been more right, for five minutes later there was a commotion at the door to the dining room, some shouts, a scuffling, a yell, and the entire room looked up, nodded in recognition, and began muttering. The waiters stiffened at the buffet where a *rijstafel* was set out, then an old Chinese man in a white jacket marched to the door and hissed something in Malay.

Flint got to his feet; the old Chinese man — whom I took to be Stanley Chee, the Head Boy — looked at Flint. Flint said, "Let that woman through." The dining room went silent as Fadila walked toward us, adjusting her blouse.

Flint pulled out a chair for her and seated her at our table.

She said, "That stupid man told me to go away — because of my feet. I said I had to see you."

"Sure you did," said Flint.

"It's important," said Fadila.

Flint looked at me, then frowned at his fingers.

I said, "We were just about to leave."

"Want to talk somewhere else?" said Flint.

Fadila said, "These people hate me. They are bad people. All Malay people are bad, and the Chinese are pigs — they eat pigs — and the Indians always cheat you. That is Ayer Hitam. It is a nasty place. I want to go far away."

Flint said, "It seems a nice quiet little place."

"No," said Fadila. "The people take you to the hospital. They want to do things to your head. They make you eat poison. If you refuse they slap you. At night they beat you with a *rotan*. They hide your clothes and make you naked so you cannot run away." She leaned toward Flint, but instead of whispering she raised her voice. "I had letters from Mr. Battley and Mr. Downs. 'Fadila is a good *amah*, Fadila speaks English, Fadila is honest.' The hospital people destroyed my letters! They cut off my hair! They beat me! I want to be your *amah*."

Flint said, "We have to go."

"Let me be your *amah*. Take me with you."

Flint's face was fixed in a smile, but his eyes were active. "Appointments. Business. At the Consulate."

"The Consulate is closed."

"*Business*," he said, and jumped to his feet.

"Take me," she said. "You are a good man. He hates

me — he thinks I am sick. But you like me. You'll let me be your *amah*." She took his arm and from the expression on Flint's face I could tell that she must be squeezing him hard. "I want to go with you."

"Outside," said Flint and started for the door with Fadila still holding tightly to his arm.

There were stares, mutters, and one clear voice: *I know what I'd do with her.* Flint hurried from the dining room. I followed, as calmly as I could, and heard, just as I left the room, one word, *Americans.*

Stanley Chee met me at the door; he bowed and made me pause. He said, "Is she troubling you? If so, I can send her away."

"Who is she?"

"Last year she was an *amok*. She was given medicine. But she will be an *amok* again soon."

"Strange," I said.

"No, not strange. Her husband took another wife, a young girl from Malacca, because Fadila did not give him any children. He went away and Fadila became an *amok*. Her husband was a devil." He straightened his gold-rimmed glasses and added, "Sir, all Malays are devils."

Flint was inside the car, Fadila outside with her face against the window, crying bitterly. I noticed that Flint had locked all the doors. I walked to the other side of the car, but he didn't unlock the door. He rolled the window down a crack and said, "This is it, old buddy. It's all yours — I've got to run. Lois is expecting me. Dinner party tonight. Keep your fingers crossed. And don't let our friend here get run over."

Fadila's face hardened as Flint drove away. She turned, limped a few feet, then faced me and said, "He is a pig and so are you."

3. White Christmas

AH CHIANG, the wife of Alec's Chinese cook, had taped bits of holly to the leaves of the potted palm. The mistletoe sprig had been knocked down by the whirling fans and was blowing across the floor under the nose of the cat, but the cotton snowflakes stuck to the mirror of the drawing room were still there. The snowflakes were Mildred's idea. She thought they made the government bungalow look festive, and there was plenty of surgical cotton in the house: Alec was a doctor at the mission hospital. And yet the decorations had a look of tropical exhaustion, shabby and temporary. The snowflakes had wilted, the holly had crinkled shut in the heat, and the mosquito coils that were burning in water-filled dishes around the room gave off a funereal aroma of incense.

It was my first Christmas in Ayer Hitam, and I was too new to the town to be able to turn down Alec's invitation. There were no cars outside when I arrived, and I thought perhaps I had got the time wrong. But I saw people at the windows and, inside, five chatting guests, three Chinese, an Indian, and a large dark woman who wore a Christmas corsage, a plastic Santa bandaged in cotton wool and red ribbon.

The Chinese — two slim girls and Reggie Woo — were whispering together in a corner. The dark woman was talking loudly to Mr. Ratnasingham. I recognized him as the pianist who had given a recital in the club lounge in November, when the Sultan had come over for the gymkhana. He was barrel-chested, a cheery Tamil with pomaded hair and an enormous wristwatch, wearing his black recital suit rather uncomfortably in the heat.

It had just rained. The sky was low, and the trees still dripped. The smell of the rain was the smell of the dampened frangipanis, a hot close perfume of muddy blossoms and a cloud of humidity that weighted the bridge of my nose. It was only after a rain that I could smell the flowers, but the rain had brought an oppressive heat to the town that made Christmas seem absurdly distant.

Mr. Ratnasingham said, "We were just talking about Midnight Mass — they have it every year at the mission."

"I always go," said the woman. "Last year there were some Eurasians there. They laughed the whole time. Disgraceful."

I guessed she had a tincture herself or she would not have mentioned their race.

"This is our American Consul," said Mr. Ratnasingham.

The woman brightened. "I knew Mr. Gilstrap very well."

Sam P. Gilstrap had been consul in Singapore in the fifties. The woman was an old-timer. I said, "Sam was half-Indian."

Mr. Ratnasingham smiled. He came close enough for me to hear his watch tick.

"Cherokee," I said.

Mr. Ratnasingham said, "What was your previous post?"

"Africa — Uganda," I said. "One year they deported half a dozen Europeans for singing *White Christmas*."

Mr. Ratnasingham laughed. "They're just down from the trees. That would never happen in Ayer Hitam."

"I mustn't drink too much," said the woman, and I was sure she was Eurasian by her scowl. "I lose my voice if I drink too much brandy."

"Miss Duckworth is in the choir," said Mr. Ratnasingham.

"So you're not the only musician, Mr. Ratnasingham."

"Please call me Francis," he said. "Actually, I'm a solicitor."

"I've always been in the Christmas choir," said Miss Duckworth.

The Chinese girls had drifted over to listen.

"We're talking about Midnight Mass," said Mr. Ratnasingham. "Are you going?"

They gave that negative cautioning Chinese bark, and one of the girls said, "Meffidist."

"Drinks, drinks — who hasn't got one?" It was Alec, with a bottle of Tiger. He pumped my hand. "I saw that enormous bottle of duty-free whiskey on the table and I knew it must be yours."

"Season's greetings."

He made a face. "I hate Christmas."

"It's going to be quite a party."

"We do it for them," he said.

More guests had begun to arrive, Dr. Estelle Lim, the botanist; Squibb and his Malay wife; Mr. Sundrum, who, half-Chinese and half-Indian, looked Malay. Alec greeted them, then went on, "We have a Christmas party every year. It's Mildred's big day." Mildred, rushing drinks to the newcomers, was a Chinese girl who looked twenty but might have been fifty; Alec had married her after settling in Ayer Hitam to supervise the hospital. "She keeps it going. They appreciate it."

I saw who they were. They weren't in the Club; they weren't of the town. Anglicized, a little ridiculous, overneat, mostly Christian, they were a small group with no local affiliations — Methodist Chinese, Catholic Indian, undeclared half-caste — the Empire's orphans. By marriage or inclination they were the misfits of the town for whom the ritual generosity of Christmas was a perfect occasion to declare themselves. From the conversations I heard it sounded as if they had not seen one another since the previous Christmas, here at the Stewarts'.

Alec said, "When they kick us out what'll they do then?"

I didn't know what to say.

He said, "There won't be any more Christmas parties."

Dr. Lim came over to where we were standing. I noticed she had a glass of beer, which interested me, because the Chinese aren't drinkers. But the others were drinking beer as well, and Squibb had a large bottle of Tiger and was refilling glasses. Dr. Lim was a tall woman with long black hair combed to the small of her back. She had that fine pale Chinese skin that is as tight and unmarked as the membrane on tropical fruit. She handed a small box to Alec and said, "Merry Christmas."

"What's this?"

"Just a present-*lah*," she said.

"I'm going to open it, my dear," said Alec, who looked slightly embarrassed. He tore off the gift-wrapping — reindeers, Santa Clauses, holly, snow — and took out a green and yellow necktie.

"Batik," she said.

"Just what I need." He kissed her on the cheek and she went away smiling. Then he said, "I haven't worn one of these bloody nooses since nineteen fifty-seven." He put it on carelessly. He was wearing a blue short-sleeved sports shirt, and the garish colors of the tie made him look as if he were drunk and toppling forward.

Hovering, the others presented their gifts. Mr. Ratnasingham gave him a calendar on a stand with a plastic antique car glued to the base; the Methodists gave Mildred some perfume, Miss Duckworth followed up with fancy handkerchiefs, and Mr. Sundrum produced a bunch of white carnations. Everyone took turns sniffing the flowers — they were regarded as quite a prize. In a country where fantastic purple and yellow orchids showed their outlandish ears and whiskers in every garden, the colorless carnation was valued as a great rarity. Dr. Lim explained how they grew them up on Fraser's Hill. Not odd, then, that we sweating foreigners should be considered so special by these dainty Malaysians; they were the orchids, we the carnations.

Squibb said, "Have a little of this," and poured me a brandy.

The natives say if you take brandy with durian fruit you die," said Reggie Woo.

"Codswallop," said Alec.

"It's what they say," said Reggie.

"I've never believed that," said Miss Duckworth.

"Who are the natives?" I asked.

"Malays," said Reggie.

"We're not natives," said Hamida Squibb. "The *sakais* are — Laruts and what not."

"There was an old man over in the *kampong*," said Mr. Sundrum. "He took two cups of brandy and then ate a durian. He died. His picture was in the *Straits Times*."

"Absolute rubbish," said Alec. Mr. Sundrum winced and went to find a vase for the carnations. Alec added in a whisper, "But mind you, I wouldn't try it myself."

"Drink up, Hamida," Squibb was saying. He lurched over to me, perspiring, and snatched at my shoulder. Brandy seemed to be percolating out of his eyes. He said, "She's a Muslim — she only drinks at Christmas."

Miss Duckworth said, "I always cry at Christmas. I can't help it."

Mildred, in her dark blue *cheongsam*, raised a sherry glass: "Merry Christmas to everyone!" This brought mutters of "The very best," "Here's to you," and "Cheers."

Ah Kwok entered from the kitchen carrying a large varnished turkey on a platter, Ah Chiang behind him with a bowl of potatoes and a gravy boat. Then Mildred flew, got Alec to carve, and set out the rest of the dishes on the long table.

Mr. Ratnasingham said, "That's a big bird."

"A sixteen-pounder," said Alec. "Mildred bought it in Singapore — Cold Storage gets them from Australia."

"Australia!" said one of the Methodists, clearly overwhelmed.

"And I remembered that you Americans like cranberry sauce," said Mildred to me.

"I adore cranberry sauce," said the other Methodist. She turned to me. "I've always wanted to go to America."

Mildred made a great show of seating us. Alec stood aside and said, "I don't care where I sit as long as it's near the gin bottle," but Mildred pushed and pointed: "No — it has to be boy-girl-boy-girl."

Hamida said, "That's the way it should be. In my *kampong* the men used to eat in one room while the women served!"

"Quite right," said Squibb. "I thought I was marrying a Malay and look what I get. Doris Archer."

"You're the Malay," said Hamida.

Mildred directed me to sit between Dr. Lim and one of the Methodist girls.

Alec said, "For what we are about to receive may we be truly grateful."

"Amen" — it chimed assertively in a dozen different voices.

Miss Duckworth said, "This reminds me of last year."

"And the year before," said Alec.

"We used to have such lovely Christmases," said Miss Duckworth. "Of course that was in Singapore. Tang's had a Santa Claus on their roof — in a sleigh with all the reindeer. And that week your Chinese provisioner would give you a Christmas basket with tins and fruit all tied in red ribbon. Then there were drinks at the Seaview Hotel and a carol service at the Cathedral. There were so many people there then."

"There are people there now," said Reggie Woo.

"I mean English people," said Miss Duckworth. "Now it's all Japanese."

Dr. Lim said, "We used to think white people smelled like cheese."

"Like corpses," said Mildred. "But it was their clothes. After they had been here for a few months they stopped smelling like dead cheese."

"I like cheese," said Reggie Woo.

"So do I!" said one of the Methodists, and everyone nodded: cheese was very good, and one day Malays, Indians, and Chinese would realize that.

"Santa Claus is still on Tang's roof, Elsie," said Mildred. "I saw it when I picked up the turkey."

"Cute," said Hamida.

"Cold Storage was decorated, too. They were playing carols on the loudspeaker system."

"But there's no one there to appreciate it," said Miss Duckworth. "No, they don't have Christmases like years ago."

"Christmas in England," said Mr. Sundrum. "That's a real white Christmas."

"Horrible," said Squibb. "You have no idea. We had a council house outside Coventry. All I remember is expecting something to happen that never happened. I didn't know my old man had been laid off."

"But the snow," said Mr. Sundrum.

"Hate it," said Squibb. "Freezes the pipes."

"I'd like to see snow," said Mr. Sundrum. "Just once. Maybe touch it."

"Ah Kwok, show Sundrum to the fridge," said Alec. "He wants to stick his hand in the freezing compartment."

Ah Kwok cackled and brought second helpings.

Dr. Lim said, "Listen — it's starting to rain."

It was; I could see the palm fronds nodding at the window, and then it began on the roof, a light patter on the tiles. It encouraged talk, cheerless and regretful, of other Christmases, of things no one had ever seen, of places they had never visited; phrases heard secondhand and mispronounced. They were like children with old inaccurate memories, preparing themselves for something that would never occur.

In that same mood, Dr. Lim said, "I had a dream last night about my father."

"I like hearing people's dreams," said Mildred.

"My father is dead," said Dr. Lim, and she gave her plate a nudge. She lit a cigarette.

"I don't think I want to hear," said one of the Methodists.

"Go on, Estelle," said Alec. "You've got us all in suspense."

"He came into my room," she said. "But he was dressed in white pajamas — Chinese ones, with those funny buttons. He was buried in clothes like that. He had something in his hand and I could tell he was very cross. Then I saw what he was holding — an opium pipe. He showed it to me and came so close I could see the tobacco stains on his teeth. I said to him, 'What do you want?' He didn't reply, but I knew what he was thinking. Somehow, he was thinking, *You're not my daughter anymore.*"

"That gives me the shivers," said Mildred.

"Then he lifted up the opium pipe and broke it in half," said Dr. Lim. "He just snapped it in my face. He was angry."

"And you woke up," said Mr. Ratnasingham.

"Yes, but that was the strange part. When I woke up he was still there in my room. The white pajamas were shining at me. I looked harder and he backed out the door."

Everyone had stopped eating. Dr. Lim puffed her cigarette, and though her face was fixed in a smile I could see no pleasure in it.

"White is the Chinese color for death," said Mr. Sundrum.

"That's what I mean," said Dr. Lim.

"Like black is for us," said Reggie Woo.

Mildred said, "I think it's time for the Christmas pudding. Alec, get your brandy butter."

Hamida said, "I don't believe in ghosts. Do you, Francis?"

"I'm a Catholic," said Mr. Ratnasingham.

Miss Duckworth had begun to cry. She cried without a sound, terribly, shaking her shoulders as if she were trying to stand up.

"Can I get you anything?" said one of the Methodists.

"No," whispered Miss Duckworth, sobbing hoarsely. "I always cry at Christmas."

The girl said, "I wasn't here last year."

Squibb said, "I used to dress up as Santa Claus. But you're all getting old now, and besides I'm drunk."

The Christmas pudding was carried alight from the kitchen by Ah Kwok, and Ah Chiang brought the cheese board. I finished my pudding quickly, and seeing me with an empty bowl, Dr. Lim passed me the cheese. She said, "You must have some of this."

"Just a slice of the brie," I said.

"That's not brie — it's camembert," said Dr. Lim.

"He doesn't know the difference!" cried Reggie Woo.

Mr. Ratnasingham said, "How about a Christmas song?" He began to sing "White Christmas" in his harsh Tamil voice. The others joined in, some drunkenly, some sweetly, drowning the sound of the rain on the bungalow roof.

"You're not singing," muttered Dr. Lim to me.

So I did, but it was awkward because only I knew the last verse, and I was obliged to sing it alone like a damned fool while the others hummed.

4. Pretend I'm Not Here

EVEN an amateur bird-watcher knows the bird from the way the empty nest is woven on a limb; and the wallpaper you hate at your new address is a pattern in the former tenant's mind. So I came to know Rogers, my predecessor at the Consulate, from the harsh-voiced people who phoned for him at odd hours and the unpaid bills that arrived to reveal his harassments so well. That desk drawer he forgot to empty told me a great deal about his hoarding postcards and the travels of his friends (Charlie and Nance in Rome, Tom and Grace in Osaka — interesting, because both couples reported "tummy-aches"). But I knew Rogers best from the habits of Peeraswami, the Indian clerk, and the descent of Miss Harbottle.

Peeraswami said, "I see European lady today morning, *Tuan*," and I knew he had no letters. Rogers had allowed him to take credit for the mail: he beamed with an especially important letter and handed it over slowly, weighing it in his brown hand like an award; if there were no letters he apologized and made conversation. Rogers must have found this behavior consoling. It drove me up the wall.

"Thank you." I went back to my report.

He hesitated. "In market. With camera. Taking snaps of City Bar's little girl." Woo Boh Swee, who owned the establishment, was known locally as City Bar, though his elder child was always called Reggie. "European from America."

"An American?" I looked up. "How do you know?"

"Wearing a hat," he said. "Carrying her own boxes."

"That doesn't mean she's an American."

"Riding the night bus." He smiled. "American."

A show of contempt from the barefoot mail-boy. Americans, once thought of as free-spenders and luxury travelers, were now considered cheapskates. What he said was partly true: the night bus from Kuala Lumpur was used mostly by American students and Tamil rubber tappers. But Peeraswami was such a know-it-all; I hoped he was wrong.

I saw her after lunch. She was sitting on the front steps of the Consulate, fiddling with her camera. Her suitcases were stacked next to her. I recognized her from the hat. It was a Mexican model, and the wide brim was tied at the sides by a blue ribbon, making it into a silly bonnet with a high conical crown.

She said, "I shouldn't be doing this in broad daylight."

She was juggling little yellow capsules, changing the film in her camera. I stepped past her and unlocked the front door.

"Are you open now?" She looked up and made a horrible face at the sun.

"No," I said. "Not until two. You've got a few minutes more."

"I'll just sit right here."

I went inside, and reflecting on that hat, considered leaving by the back door. But it was too hot for tennis, too early for a drink; and I had work to do. I turned on the fan and began signing the letters I'd dictated that morning. I had signed only three when the door burst open.

"Hey!" She was at the door, undoing her bonnet. "Where's Mr. Rogers?"

"I'm the new Consul."

"Why didn't you say so out there?"

"I only admit to it during office hours," I said. "It cuts down on the work." I showed her my pen, the letters on my blotter.

"Well, I've got a little problem," she said. Now her bonnet was off, and I could see her face clearly. She was sunburned, plump, and not young; her hands were deeply freckled and she stood leaning one fist on my desk, talking to me as if at an employee. "It's to do with accommodation. I don't have any, and I was counting on Rogers. I know him from Riyadh."

"He's in Turkey now," I said. "But there's a rest house in town."

"It's full."

"There are two Chinese hotels."

She leaned still further on her fist: "Did you ever spend a night in a Chinese hotel?"

"There's a campsite," I said. "If you know anything about camping."

"I camped my way through the Great Nafud. That's where I met Rogers," she said. "I wrote a book about it."

"Then Ayer Hitam shouldn't bother you in the least."

"My tent was stolen yesterday in K.L., at the bus depot."

"You have to be careful."

"It was stolen by an American."

She looked as if she was holding me responsible. I said, "I'll keep an eye out for it. In the meantime — "

"All I want is a few square feet to throw my sleeping bag," she said. "You won't even know I'm there. And don't worry — I'll give you an acknowledgment in my book."

"You're writing another one, are you?"

"I always do."

It might have been the heat or the fact that I had just noticed she was a stout woman in late middle age and looked particularly plain and vulnerable in her faded cotton dress, with her sunburned arms and peeling nose and a bulbous bandage on her thumb. I said, "All right then. Be at my house at six and I'll see what I can fix up for you."

Ah Wing met me in the driveway as Abubaker swung the car to a halt. Ah Wing had been Rogers's cook, and he was old enough to have been cook for Rogers's predecessor as well; he had the fatigued tolerance of the Chinese employee who treats his employers as cranky birds of passage. He said, "There is a *mem* in the garden."

"Wearing a hat?"

"Wearing."

She had spread a ground sheet on the grass and opened one of her suitcases. A half-rolled sleeping bag lay on the ground sheet, and she was seated on the second suitcase, blowing up a rubber air mattress. She took the nozzle out of her mouth and said, "Hi there!"

"You're not going to sleep here, are you?"

"This suits me fine," she said. "I'm no sissy." The implication being that I was one for using a bed. "Now you just leave me be and pretend I'm not here. Don't worry about me."

"It's the grass I'm worried about," I said. "New turf. Rather frail."

She allowed herself to be persuaded, and gathered up her camping equipment. Inside the house she said, "You live like a king! Is this all yours?"

"It's rented from the Sultan."

"Taxpayers' money," she said, touching the walls as she went along.

"This is considered a hardship post by the State Department."

"I haven't seen any hardships yet," she said.

"You haven't been in town very long," I said.

"Good point," she said.

She was in the bedroom; she dropped her suitcases and sat on the bed and bounced. "A real bed!"

"I suppose you'll be wanting dinner?"

"No, sir!" She reached for her handbag. "I've got all I need right here." She took out a wilted branch of rambutans, half a loaf of bread, and a tin of Ma-Ling stew.

"That won't be necessary," I said.

"Whatever you say." On the verandah she said, "You do all right for yourself," and punished the gin bottle; and over dinner she said, "Golly, do you eat like this every day?"

I made noncommittal replies, and then I remembered. I said, "I don't even know your name."

"Harbottle," she said. "Margaret Harbottle. Miss. I'm sure you've seen my travel books."

"The name rings a bell."

"The Great Nafud was the toughest one. Rogers didn't have a place like this!"

"It must be very difficult for a woman to travel in Saudi Arabia."

"I didn't go as a woman," she said.

"How interesting."

"I went as a man," she said. "Oh, it's really quite simple. I'm ugly enough. I cut my hair and wore a burnous. They never knew the difference!"

She went on to tell me of her other travels, which were stories of cheerful privations, how she had lived on dates and Nile water for a week in Juba, slept in a ditch in Kenya, crossed to Lamu by dhow. She was eating the whole time she spoke, jabbing her fork in the air as if spearing details. "You won't believe this," she said, "but I haven't paid for a meal since Penang, and *that* was a misunderstanding."

"I believe it."

She looked out the window at the garden. "I'm going to paint that. Put it in the book. I always illustrate my own books. 'With illustrations by the author.' "

We finished dinner and I said, "I usually read at this time of day."

"Don't let me interrupt your routine," she said.

We had coffee, and then I picked up my novel. She sat in the lounge with me, smoking a Burmese cheroot, looking around the room. She said, "Boy, you do all right!" I glanced up in annoyance. "Go ahead — read," she said. "Pretend I'm not here."

Days later she was still with me. Ah Wing complained that her food was stinking up the bedroom. There was talk of her at the Club: she had been seen sniffing around the Sultan's summer house, and then had come to the club bar and made a scene when she was refused a drink. She got one eventually by saying she was my houseguest. I signed the chits the next day: five gins and a port and lemon. It must have been quite an evening.

Her worst offense was at the river. I heard the story from Peeraswami. She had gone there late one afternoon and found some men bathing, and she had begun photographing them. They had seen her but, stark naked, they couldn't run out of the water. They had shouted. She photographed that. It was only when she started away that the men wrapped themselves in sarongs and chased her, but she had taken one of their bicycles and escaped.

"They think I haven't seen a man before," she said, when I asked her about it.

"Malay men are modest," I said.

"Believe me, they've got something to be modest about!"

I decided to change the subject. I said, "I'm having some people over tomorrow for drinks."

"I don't mind," she said.

"I was hoping you wouldn't."

"And don't worry about me," she said. "Just pretend I'm not here."

I was tempted to say, "How?" I resisted and said, "You don't do much painting."

"The light's not right."

The next evening she had changed into a clean dress. I could not think of a polite way of getting rid of her. She stayed, drank more than anyone, and talked nonstop of her travels. When the guests left, she said, "They were nice, but kind of naive, you know what I mean?"

"Miss Harbottle," I said, "I'm expecting some more people this weekend."

She smiled. "Pretend I'm not here."

"That is not a very easy thing to do," I said. "You see, they're staying overnight, and I was planning to put them in your room."

"But you have lots of rooms!"

"I expect lots of guests."

"Then I'll sleep on the grass," she said. "I intended to do that anyway. You won't even know I'm there."

"But if we decide to play croquet we might disturb that nap you always have after lunch."

"It's your meals," she said. "I usually don't eat so much. But I hate to see food go to waste."

That was Thursday. On Friday I had a visit from Ali Mohammed. "It is about your houseguest," he said. "She took some cloth from my shop and has not paid for it."

"She might have forgotten."

"That is not all. The men she photographed at the river

are still cross. They want very much to break up her camera. And Mekmal says she scratched his pushbike."

"You'll have to see her about it."

"This is serious," he said, glowering and putting on his *songkok*. "She is your houseguest."

"She won't be much longer."

I can't say I was sorry her inconvenience extended to Ali Mohammed; he had been in the habit of saying to me, "When is *Tuan* Rogers coming back?" And then it occurred to me that an unwelcome guest is like a weapon. I could use Miss Harbottle quite blamelessly against Ali or Peeraswami, both of whom deserved her. An unwelcome guest could carry annoyance to your enemy; you only had to put them in touch.

"Ali Mohammed was in the office today," I said over lunch. "He says you took some cloth from him without paying for it."

"I thought it was a present."

"He didn't think so."

"When I go to a country," said Miss Harbottle, with a note of instruction in her voice, "I expect to be given presents. I'm writing a book about this place. I'm *promoting* these people."

"That reminds me," I said. "I've decided to charge you rent."

Miss Harbottle's face fell. "I never pay," she said. "I don't carry much cash." She squinted at me. "That's pretty unfair."

"I don't want money," I said.

She said, "You should be ashamed of yourself. I'm fifty-two years old."

"And not that either," I said. "Your payment will be a picture. One of your water colors for every night you stay here from now on."

"I can't find my brushes."

"I'll buy you some new ones."

"I see," she said, and as soon as we finished eating she went to her room.

Late that same night the telephone rang. It was Peeraswami. He had just come from a meeting outside the mosque. Ali Mohammed was there, and Mekmal, and City Bar, and the men from the river, the rubber tappers — everyone with a grievance against Miss Harbottle. They had discussed ways of dealing with the woman. The Malays wanted to humiliate her; the Chinese suggested turning the matter over to a secret society; the Indians had pressed for some expensive litigation. It was the first time I had seen the town united in this way, their single object — the plump Miss Harbottle — inspiring in them a sense of harmonious purpose. I didn't discourage Peeraswami, though he reported the proceedings with what I thought was uncalled-for glee.

"I'm afraid there's nothing I can do," I said. She was Rogers's guest, not mine; Rogers's friends could deal with her.

"What to do?" asked Peeraswami.

"Whatever you think best," I said. "And I wouldn't be a bit surprised if she was on the early bus tomorrow."

In the morning, Ah Wing woke me with tea and the news that there were twenty people in the garden demanding to see me. I took my time dressing and then went out. They saw me and called out in Malay, "Where is she? Where is the *orang puteh*?"

Ah Wing shook his head. He said, "Not here."

"Liar!" Peeraswami yelled, and this cry was taken up by the others.

Ah Wing turned to me and said, "She left early — on the Singapore bus."

"Liar!" said Peeraswami again. "We were at the bus station!"

"Yes," said Ali Mohammed. "There was no woman at the

station." He had a stick in his hand; he shook it at me and said, "We want to search your house."

"Wait," I said. "Did you see a European?"

"A man only," said Ali Mohammed.

"A fat one," said Peeraswami with anger and disgust. "He refused Mekmal to carry his boxes."

I'm sure my laughter bewildered them; I was full of gratitude for Miss Harbottle. I loved her for that.

5. Loser Wins

THE INSECTS warbled at the windows, and on the wall a pale gecko chattered and flicked its tail. It was one of those intimate late-night pauses — we had been drinking for two hours and had passed the point of drunken chitchat. Then, to break the silence, I said, "I've lost my spare pair of glasses."

"I hadn't noticed," said Strang. A surveyor, he had the abrupt manner of one who works alone. He was mapping this part of the state and he had made Ayer Hitam his base. His wife, Milly, was devoted to him, people said; it seemed an unusual piece of praise. Strang picked up his drink. "You won't find them."

"It's an excuse to go down to Singapore for a new pair."

Strang looked thoughtful. I expected him to say something about Singapore. We were alone. Stanley Chee had slammed the door for the last time and had left a tray of drinks on the bar that we could sign for on the chit-pad.

Still Strang didn't reply. The ensuing silence made my sentence about Singapore a frivolous echo. He walked over and poured himself a large gin, emptied a bottle of tonic into the tall glass and pinched a new slice of lemon into it.

"I ever tell you about the Parrishes?"

A rhetorical question: he was still talking.

"Married couple I met up in Kota Bharu. Jungle bashers.

Milly and I lived there our first year — looked like paradise to us, if you could stand the sand flies. Didn't see much of the Parrishes. They quarreled an awful lot, so we stayed as far away as possible from their arguments. Seemed unlucky. We'd only been married a few months." He smiled. "Old Parrish took quite a shine to Milly."

"What did the Parrishes argue about?" Was this what he wanted me to ask? I hoped he was not expecting me to drag the story out of him. I wanted him to keep talking and let it flow over me. But even at the best of times Strang was no spellbinder; tonight he seemed agitated.

"See, that shows you've never been spliced," he said. "Married people argue about everything — anything. A tone of voice, saying please, the color of the wallpaper, something you forgot, the speed of the fan, food, friends, the weather. That tie of yours — if you had a wife she'd hate you for it. A bone of contention," said Strang slowly, "is just a bone."

"Perhaps I have that in store for me." I filled my own drink and signed for that and Strang's.

"Take my advice," he said. "No — it was something you said a minute ago. Oh, you lost your specs. That's what I was going to say. The Parrishes argued about everything, but most of all they argued about things they lost. I mean, things *she* lost. She was incredible. At first he barely noticed it. She lost small things, lipstick, her cigarettes, her comb. She didn't bother to look for them. She was very county — her parents had money, and she had a kind of contempt for it. Usually she didn't even try to replace the things she lost. The funny thing is, she seemed to do it on purpose — to lose things she hated.

"He was the local magistrate. An Outward Bound type. After a week in court he was dead keen to go camping. Old Parrish — he looked like a goat, little pointed beard and those sort of hairy ears. They went on these camping trips and invariably she lost something en route — the house keys, her watch, the matches, you name it. But she was a terrific map-reader and he was appalling, so he really depended on her. I think he had some love for her. He was a lot older than she was — he'd married her on a long leave.

"Once, he showed how much he loved her. She lost fifty dollars. Not a hard thing to do — it was a fifty-dollar note, the one with the mosque on it. I would have cried, myself, but she just shrugged, and knowing how she was continually losing things he was sympathetic. 'Poor thing,' he says, 'you must feel a right charlie.' But not a bit of it. She had always had money. She didn't take a blind bit of notice, and she was annoyed that he pitied her for losing the fifty sheets. Hated him for noticing it.

"They went off on their camping trips — expeditions was more like it — and always to the same general area. Old Parrish had told me one or two things about it. There was one of these up-country lakes, with a strange island in the middle of it. They couldn't find it on the map, but they knew roughly where it was supposed to be — there's never been a detailed survey done of the Malaysian interior. But that's where the Parrishes were headed every weekend during that dry season. The attraction was the monkeys. Apparently, the local *sakais* — they might have been Laruts — had deported some wild monkeys there. The monkeys got too stroppy around the village, so being peace-loving buggers the *sakais* just caught them and tied them up and brought them to the island where they wouldn't bother anyone. There were about a dozen of these beasts, surrounded by water. An island of wild monkeys — imagine landing there on a dark night!

"In the meantime, we saw the Parrishes occasionally in the compound during the week and that's where I kept up to date with the story. As I say, his first reaction when she lost things was to be sympathetic. But afterward, it irritated him. She lost her handbag and he shouted at her. She lost her watch — it was one he had given her — and he wouldn't speak to her for days. She mislaid the bathplug, lost some jewelry, his passport disappeared. And that's the way it went — bloody annoying. I don't know what effect this had on her. I suppose she thought she deserved his anger. People who lose things get all knotted up about it, and the fear of losing things makes them do it all the more. That's what I thought then.

"And the things she lost were never found. It was uncanny, as if she just wished them away. He said she didn't miss them.

"Then, on one of these expeditions she lost the paraffin. Doesn't seem like much, but the place was full of leeches and a splash of paraffin was the only thing that'd shake them loose from your arms or legs. They both suffered that weekend and didn't find the island either. Then, the next weekend, she lost the compass, and that's when the real trouble started. Instead of pitying her, or getting angry, or ignoring it, old Parrish laughed. He saw how losing the compass inconvenienced her in her map-reading, and she was so shaken by that horrible laugh of his she was all the more determined to do without it. She succeeded, too. She used a topographical map and somehow found the right landmarks and led them back the way they'd come.

"But Parrish still laughed. I remember the day she lost the car keys — *his* car keys, mind you, because she'd lost practically everything she owned and now it was his stuff up the spout. You could hear old Parrish halfway to Malacca. Then it was the malaria tablets. Parrish laughed even harder — he said he'd been in the Federation so long he was immune to it, but being young and new to the place she'd get a fever, and he found that screamingly funny. This was too much for her, and when his wedding ring went missing — God only knows how *that* happened — and Parrish just laughed, that was the last straw. I suppose it didn't help matters when Parrish set off for the courthouse in the morning saying, 'What are you going to lose today, my darling?'

"Oh, there was much more. He talked about it at parties, laughing his head off, while she sulked in a corner, and we expected to find him dead the next morning with a knitting-needle jammed through his wig.

"But, to make a long story short, they went off on one of their usual expeditions. No compass, no Paludrine, no torch — she'd lost practically everything. By this time, they knew their way, and they spent all that Saturday bushwhacking through the *ulu*. They were still headed in that deliberate way of theirs for the monkey island, and now I remember that a lot of people called him 'Monkey' Parrish. She claimed it was mythical, didn't exist, except in the crazy fantasies of a lot of *sakais*; but Monkey said, 'I know what you've done with it, my darling — you've lost that island!' And naturally he laughed.

"They were making camp that night in a grove of bamboos when it happened. It was dusk, and looking up they saw one of those enormous clouds of flying foxes in the sky. Ever see them? They're really fruit-bats, four feet from tip to tip, and they beat the air slowly. You get them in the *ulu* near the coast. Eerie, they are — scare the wits out of you the way they fly, and they're ugly as old boots. You can tell the old ones by the way they move, sort of dropping behind and losing altitude while the younger ones push their noses on ahead. It's one of the weirdest sights in this country, those flying foxes setting off in the twilight, looking so fat and fearsome in the sky. Like a bad dream, a kind of monster film — they come out of nowhere.

"She said, 'Look, they're heading for that island.'

"He said, 'Don't be silly — they're flying east, to the coast.'

" 'There's the light,' she said, 'that's west.' She claimed the bats preferred islands and would be homing in on one where there was fruit — monkey food. The wild monkeys slept at night, so they wouldn't bother the bats. She said, 'I'm going to have a look.'

" 'There's no torch,' he says, and he laughs like hell.

" 'There's a moon,' she says. And without another word she's crashing through the bamboos in the direction the foxes are flying. Parrish — Monkey Parrish — just laughed and sat down by the fire to have a pipe before bed. Can you see him there, chuckling to himself about this wife of his who loses everything, how he suddenly realizes that she's lost herself and he has a fit of laughter? Great hoots echoing through the jungle as old Parrish sees he's rid of her at last!

"Maybe. But look at it another way. The next morning he wakes up and sees she's not there. She never came back. At first he slaps his thigh and laughs and shouts, 'She's lost!' Then he looks around. No map, no compass, no torch — only that low dense jungle that stretches for hundreds of miles across the top of the country, dropping leeches on anyone who's silly enough to walk through it. And the more he thinks about it the more it becomes plain to him that *he*'s the one who's lost — she's wished him away, like the wedding ring and the torch and the fifty-dollar bill. Suddenly he's not laughing anymore.

"I'm only guessing. I don't really know what he was thinking. I had the story from her, just before she left the country. She said there were only two monkeys on the island, a male and a female, bickering the whole time, like her and her late husband. Yes, *late* husband. No one ever found him — certainly not her, but she wouldn't, would she?"

6. The Flower of Malaya

"Is SHE one of yours?" they'd ask on the club verandah when a white girl went past. Nothing salacious intended: they were just wondering if she was American. It was in this way — a casual inquiry to which I did not have an answer — that I discovered Linda Clem. We assigned names to strangers, a tropical pastime, nicknaming them at a distance; she was "The Flower of Malaya." For a brief period I found it hard to think of her and not be reminded of that disappointed ghost the Malays believe in, who is known simply as Pontianak, "The Ghost." Pontianak has a pretty face and is always alone. She takes a trishaw, but when it arrives at the destination and the driver asks for the fare, the seat is empty, Pontianak is gone. Or she stops a man on a jungle path — something Malay women never do — and asks the man to follow her. The offer is not usually refused, but when she turns to go the man sees she has an enormous hole in her back. Then she melts away. At night, before heavy storms, she can be heard weeping in the banana groves. Pontianak is the ghost of a woman who died in childbirth and she has been sighted from Kota Bharu on the north coast to Kukup in the south; the Javanese know her, so do the Sumatrans. She gets around, but what does she want?

Linda Clem got around, and she had Pontianak's melancholy. It seems to come easily to most women — there is a kind of sisterhood in sadness. She was a teacher. That word, so simple at home, spells disaster in the East. They have such hopes, and it always ends so badly. She taught English, most of them do, never asking themselves what happens when a half-starved world is mumbling in heavily accented English, "I want — ." She struck me as accident-prone, but I suppose that was her job, her nationality, her boyfriend.

She was a plump graceless soul who hated her body. She had fat legs and a bottom only a Chinese upholsterer could have admired. But she had a pretty face with slightly magnified features, and she had long beautiful hair. Within a week of arriving she was in a sarong — ill-fitting, but it took care of those legs. Within a month she was on the arm of a boy vaguely related to the Sultan, a cousin of a cousin, known locally (but inaccurately) as "Tunku," The Prince. He was a charming idle fellow who owed money at every Chinese shop in town.

A hopeless liaison: he wanted to be American, she aimed at being Malay — the racial somersault often mistaken for tolerance. It was usually inverted bigotry, ratting on your own race. I saw their determined effort at affection, strolling hand-in-hand across the maidan, or at the club social evenings — evidently she thought she was teaching us a thing or two about integration; and at City Bar, smooching under the gaze of the Chinese secret society that congregated there. I guessed The Prince was using her money — she looked credulous enough to loan it to him. How pathetic to watch the newcomer, innocent to the deceits of the East, making all the usual mistakes.

I waited for the eventual break-up, but it happened sooner than I expected. One morning she appeared at the Consulate just after we opened. She pushed Peeraswami aside, ignored the secretary's squawk, and flung open my office door.

"I'm looking for the Consul," she said.

"Do you have an appointment?" I asked.

"The secretary already asked me that," she said. "Look, this is an emergency."

She sat down and threw her shoulder bag on a side table. Is it only Americans who treat consulates as their personal property, and diplomatic personnel as their flunkies? "They move in and walk all over you," a colleague used to say — he kept his door locked against American nationals demanding service. It earned us, in Ayer Hitam, the contemptuous pity of the European consulates.

Miss Clem said, "I want to report a break-in."

"I'm afraid that's a matter for the police."

"This is confidential."

"They can keep a secret," I said.

"You're my consul," she said rather fiercely. "I'm not going to any Malay cop." She was silent a moment, then she said, "A man's been in my room."

I said nothing. She glared at me.

"You don't care, do you?"

"I find it hard to understand your alarm, Miss Clem."

"So you know my name." She frowned. "They told me you were like that."

"Let's try to be constructive, shall we?" I said. "What exactly did the man do?"

"You want details," she said disgustedly.

"Isn't that why you came here?"

"I told you why I came here."

"You'll have to be specific. Are you reporting a theft?"

"No."

"Assault?"

"Kinda."

"Miss Clem," I said, and I was on the point of losing my temper, "I'm very busy. I can't read your mind and I'd rather you didn't waste my time. Now play ball!"

She put her face in her hands and began to blubber, clownish notes of hooted grief. She had that brittle American composure that breaks all at once, like a windshield shattered with a pebble. A fat girl crying is an appalling sight, in any case, all that motion and noise. Finally she spoke up: "I've been raped!"

I closed the door to the outer office, and said, "Do you know who did it?"

She nodded sadly and pushed her hair out of her eyes. She said, "Ibrahim."

"The Prince?"

"He's no prince," she said. Then plaintively, "After all I did for him."

"You'll have to go to the police and make a statement."

"What will I say?" she said in a small voice.

"Just tell them what happened."

"Oh, God, it was really awful," she said. "He came through the window with no clothes on — just like that. I was up combing my hair and I saw him in the mirror. He turned off the light and grabbed me by the arm. I tried to push him away, but you know, it was really strange — he was all slippery. His skin was covered by some kind of oil. 'Cut it out,' I said. But he wouldn't. He didn't say anything. He just lifted me up by the legs like a wheelbarrow, and — I'll never forgive him for this. I was giving him English lessons!"

"Tell that to the police. I'll send you in my car. They'll want to know the times and that sort of thing."

"What'll they do?"

"I imagine they'll arrest him, if they can find him."

"They'll find him," she said bitterly. "I just saw him in town."

So Ibrahim, The Prince, was picked up, and Miss Clem pressed charges. Only the younger members of the Club wondered why The Prince had stayed around. The rest of us knew how Miss Clem had ventured into danger; she had led him on and the poor dumb Malay had misread all her signs. Miss Clem had discovered how easy it was, after all, to be a Malay. It was typical enough for farce.

Squibb said, "She got just what she deserved. She was asking for it."

"She doesn't know the first thing about it," said Strang.

Squibb squinted maliciously: "She knows now. The Flower of Malaya's been deflowered."

I said I agreed with them — it was fatal to disagree with anyone in such a small post — but I sympathized with the girl. She knew nothing of the country; she had fallen in headfirst. All you had to do to survive was practice elementary caution. In one sense she deserved what she got, but it was a painful lesson. I had some sympathy for The Prince, too; he was not wholly to blame. He had mistaken her for one of his own. But how was he to know? They were all beginners, that was the worst of these interracial tangles: how infantile they were!

Predictably, Miss Clem stopped wearing her sarong. She tied her hair differently, and she began dropping into the Club alone. The members were kind to her — I noticed she usually had a tennis partner, and that was truly an act of kindness, since she was such a dreadful player. Overnight, she acquired the affectations of a memsahib; a bit sharp with the waiters and ball-boys, a common parody of hauteur in her commands, that odd exaggerated play-actor's laugh, and a posture I associate with a woman who is used to being waited on — a straight-backed rigidity with formal, irritated hand signals to the staff, as if her great behind was cemented to a plinth. Then I disliked her, and I saw how she was patronized by the club bores, who rehearsed their ill-natured stories with her. She encouraged them in racial innuendo; the memsahib lapping at the double peg in her glass. A month before she had been sidling up to a Malay and probably planning to take out citizenship; now she was in a high-backed Malacca chair under a fan calling out, "Boy!"

There was, so far, no trial. Ibrahim the Prince was languishing in the Central Jail, while the lawyers collected evidence. But they hadn't extracted a confession from him, and that was the most unusual feature of the whole business, since even an innocent man would own up simply to get a night's sleep. The Ayer Hitam police were not noted for their gentleness with suspects.

One night at the Club Miss Clem spoke to me in her new actressy voice. "I want to thank you for all you've done. I'm glad it's over."

"You're welcome," I said, "but I'm afraid it's not over yet. There's still the trial. You won't like that."

"I hope you'll be there to give me moral support."

"I don't like circuses," I said. "But if there's anything useful I can do, let me know."

The following week she had a different story, a different voice. She entered the Consulate as she had that first time, pushing my staff aside and bursting into my office. She had been crying, and I could see she was out of breath.

"You're not going to believe this," she said. Not the memsahib now, but that other voice of complaint, the innocent surprised. She sat down. "It happened again."

"Another break-in?"

"I was raped," she said softly.

"The Prince is in jail," I said in gentle contradiction.

"I'm telling you I was raped!" she shouted, and I was sure she could be heard all the way to the Club.

"Well, who do you suppose could have done it?"

She said nothing; she lowered her eyes and sniffed.

"Tell me, Miss Clem," I said, "does this sort of thing happen to you often?"

"What do you mean 'often'?"

"Do you find that when you're alone, in a strange place, people get it in their heads to rape you? Perhaps you have something that drives men wild, some hidden attraction."

"You don't believe me. I knew you wouldn't."

"It seems rather extraordinary."

"It happened again. I'm not making it up." Then she pulled the top of her dress across one shoulder and showed me, just below her shoulder bone, a plum-colored bruise. I looked closer and saw circling it were the stitch-marks of a full set of teeth.

"You should have that seen to," I said.

"I want that man caught," she insisted.

"I thought we *had* caught him."

"So did I."

"So it wasn't The Prince?"

"I don't know," she said.

"Was it the same man as before?"

"Yes, just like before. He was terrible — he laughed."

And her story was the same, even the same image as before, about him picking her legs up "like a wheelbarrow," a rather chilling caricature of sexuality. Truth is not a saga of alarming episodes; it is a detail, a small clear one, that gives a fiction life. Hers was that horrible item, unusual enough to be a fact and too bizarre to be made up, about the slippery skin of the rapist. He was greasy, slimy — his whole body gleamed. She couldn't fight against him; she couldn't get a grip on him. He had appeared in her room and pounced on her, and she was helpless. This time she said she had resisted and it was only by biting on her that he held on.

I said, "You'll have to drop your charges against The Prince."

"I'm afraid to."

"But don't you see? He's in jail, and if it was the same man as before then it couldn't have been The Prince."

"I don't know what to do."

"I suggest you get a telephone installed in your house. If you hear any suspicious noises, ring me or the police. Obviously it's some local person who fancies you."

But The Prince was not released. Somehow the police had extracted a confession from him, a date was set for the trial and Miss Clem was scheduled to testify. That was weeks away. In the meantime, Miss Clem had her telephone put in. She rang me one evening shortly afterward.

"Is there anything wrong?" I asked, hearing her voice.

"Everything's fine," she said. "I was just testing it."

"From now on only ring me in the event of an emergency," I said.

"I think I'm going to be all right," she said, and rang off.

For a brief period I forgot about Miss Clem, the Flower of Malaya. I had enough to keep me busy — visa matters were a continual headache. It was about this time that the Strangs got their divorce — which is another story — but the speculation at the Club, up to then concerned with Miss Clem, was centered on what Milly Strang could possibly be doing in Bali. She had sent a gleeful postcard to Angela, but nothing to Lloyd. Miss Clem dropped from view.

My opposite number came down from Penang on a private

visit and we had a little reception for him. The invitation specified "drinks 6–8 P.M." but at eleven there were still people on the verandah badgering the waiters for fresh drinks. My reaction was tactical: I went into my study and read the cables. Usually it worked — when the host disappears the guests are at sea; they get worried and invariably they take the hint.

The telephone rang. I was not quick and when I picked up the receiver the line went dead. At first I did nothing; then I remembered and was out the door.

Peeraswami had been helping out at the party. As I rushed out the back door I noticed him at the edge of the courtyard, chatting to the kitchen staff. I called to him and told him to get into the car. On the way I explained where we were going, but I did not say why.

Miss Clem's house was in the teachers' compound of the mission school. It was in darkness. I jammed on the brakes and jumped out. Peeraswami was right behind me. From the bungalow I could hear Miss Clem sobbing.

"Go around back," I said to Peeraswami. "In those trees. If you see anyone, catch him!"

Peeraswami sprinted away. I went into the house and stumbled in the direction of the sobbing. Miss Clem was alone, sitting on the edge of the bed. I switched on the light and saw her sad fat body on the rumpled bedclothes. She had an odd shine, a gloss on her skin that was lit like a snail's track. But it covered her stomach; it was too viscous to be perspiration and it had the smell of jungle. She was smeared with it, and though she seemed too dazed to notice it, it was like nothing I had ever seen before. She lay down sobbing and pulled a sheet over her.

"It was him," she said.

"The Prince?"

"No, no! Poor Ibrahim," she sobbed.

"Take a bath," I said. "You can come back to my house when you've changed."

"Where are you going?"

"I've got to find my *peon.*"

I found him hurrying back to the house. In the best of times he had a strange face, his dark skin and glittering teeth, his close-set eyes and on his forehead a thumbprint of ashes, the Eye of God. He was terrified — not a rare thing in Peeraswami, but terror on that Tamil face was enough to frighten anyone else.

"*Tuan!*" he cried.

"Did you see him?"

"Yes, yes," he said. "He had no clothings, no shirtings. Bare-naked!"

"Well, why the hell didn't you catch him?" I snapped.

"*Tuan,*" said Peeraswami, "no one can catch *Orang Minyak.*"

"You knew him?"

"Everyone know him."

"I don't understand," I said. "*Orang* is man. But *Minyak* — is that a name?"

"It his name. *Minyak* — oily, like ghee butter on his body. You try but you cannot catch hold. He trouble the girls, only the girls at night. But he Malay spirit — not Indian, *Malay,*" said Peeraswami, as if disclaiming any responsibility for another race's demons.

An incubus, I thought. What a fate for the Flower of Malaya. Peeraswami lingered. He could see I was angry he hadn't caught *Orang Minyak.* And even then I only half-believed.

"Well, you did your best," I said, and reached out to shake his hand. I squeezed and his hand shot away from mine, and then my own hand was slippery, slick, and smelling of jungle decay.

"I touch, but I do not catch," said Peeraswami. He stooped and began wiping his palms on the grass. "You see? No one can catch *Orang Minyak*."

7. The Autumn Dog

"MINE used to sweat in his sleep," said the woman in the white dress, a bit drunkenly. "It literally poured off him! During the day he'd be dry as a bone, but as soon as he closed his eyes, bingo, he'd start percolating."

Her name was Maxine Stanhope and practically the first thing she had said to the woman who sat opposite was, "Please call me Max, all my friends do." They sat on the verandah of a hotel outside Denpasar, in Bali, in the sun the other tourists avoided. They had dark reptilian tans and slouched languorously in the comfortable chairs like lizards sunning themselves on a rock. Lunch was over, the wine was gone, their voices were raised in emphatic friendliness. They had known each other for only three hours.

"Mine didn't sweat that much, but he made the most fantastic noises," said Milly Strang. "He carried on these mumbling monologues, using different voices, and groaning and sort of swallowing. Sometimes I'd wake up and just look at him and laugh."

"It's not funny," said Maxine. But she was laughing; she was the larger of the two, and sharp-featured, her hair tugged back and fitting her head closely. There was a male's growl of satisfaction in her laugh, not the high mirth you would have expected from that quick, companionable mouth. "When I remember the things he put me through, I think I must have been crazy. Mine made me warm his cup. I should have broken it over his head."

"Mine had this way of pawing me when he was feeling affectionate. He was really quite strong. He left bruises! I suppose he thought he was — what's the expression? — turning me on."

"They always think that," said Maxine. She held the empty wine bottle over the other's glass until a drop fell out. "Let's have another — wine makes me honest."

"I've had quite enough," said Milly.

"You're the boss," said Maxine. Then she said, "Mine weighed two hundred pounds."

"Well, mine was at least that. I'm not exaggerating. When I think of him on top of me — it's ludicrous."

"It's obscene. Mine kept gaining weight, and finally I said to him, 'Look, if this goes on any more we won't be able to make love.' Not that *that* worried me. By then I'd already taken a lover — not so much a lover as a new way of life. But Erwin said it didn't matter whether you were fat or thin. If you were fat you'd just find a new position."

"The fat man's position!"

"Exactly. And he got this — this manual. All the positions were listed, with little diagrams and arrows. Arrows! It was like fitting a plug, an electrical manual for beginners. 'Here,' he said, 'I think that one would suit us.' They all had names — I forget what that one was, but it was the fat man's position. Can you imagine?"

"Mine had manuals. Well, he called them manuals. They were Swedish I think. You must have seen them. Interesting and disgusting at the same time. He didn't want me to see them — I mean, he hid them from me. Then I found them and he caught me going through them. Honestly, I think I gave him quite a shock. He looked over my shoulder. 'Ever see anything like it?' he said. I could hear him breathing heavily. He was getting quite a thrill!"

"Did yours make a fuss over the divorce?"

"No," said Milly, "what about yours?"

"*He* divorced *me*. Nothing in particular — just a whole series of things. But, God, what a messy business. It dragged on for months and months."

"Mine was over before I knew it."

"Lucky," said Maxine.

"Up till then we'd been fairly happy."

"Happy marriages so-called turn into really messy divorces," said Maxine.

"I think not," said Milly. "The best marriages end quickly."

Theirs, the Strangs', had gone on serenely for years, filling us with envious contempt. It fell to pieces in an afternoon of astonishing abuse. They had pretended politeness for so long only an afternoon was necessary. Then we were friendlier toward the couple, no longer a couple, but Milly alone in the house and Lloyd at the Club. The marriages in Ayer Hitam were no frailer than anywhere else, but we expatriates knew each other well and enjoyed a kind of kinship. A divorce was like a death in the family. Threatened with gloom, we became thoughtful. The joking was nervous: Milly had burned the toast; Lloyd had made a pass at the *amah*. Afterward, Lloyd clung to the town. He was overrehearsed. One of his lines went, "It was our ages. Out of the horse latitudes and into the roaring forties." He was no sailor; he was taking it badly.

Milly, unexpectedly cheerful, packed her bags and left the compound. Within a week she was in Indonesia. Before she left she had said to Angela Miller, "I always wanted to go to

Bali. Lloyd wouldn't let me." She went, Lloyd stayed, and it looked as if he expected her back: her early return to Ayer Hitam would have absolved him of all blame.

It did not happen that way. Before long, we all knew her story. Milly saw friends in Djakarta. The friends were uneasy with this divorced woman in their house. They sent their children out to play and treated her the way they might have treated a widow, with a mixture of somberness and high spirits, fearing the whole time that she'd drink too much and burst into tears. Milly found their hospitality exhausting and went to Djokjakarta, for the temples. Though tourists (seeing her eating alone) asked her to join them, she politely refused. How could she explain that she liked eating alone and reading in bed and waking when she wished and doing nothing? Life was so simple, and marriage only a complication. Marriage also implied a place: you were married and lived in a particular house; unmarried, you lived in the world, and there were no answers required of you. Milly changed her status slowly, regaining an earlier state of girlishness from the widowhood of divorce. Ten years was returned to her, and more than that, she saw herself granted a valuable enlightenment, she was wiser and unencumbered, she was free.

The hotel in Bali, which would have been unthinkably expensive for a couple with a land surveyor's income, was really very cheap for one person. She told the manager (Swiss, married — she could tell at a glance) she would stay a month. There was a column in the hotel register headed *Destination*. She left it blank. The desk clerk indicated this. "I haven't got one," she said, and she surprised the man with her natural laugh.

The tourists, the three-day guests at the hotel, the ones with planes to catch were middle-aged; some were elderly, some infirm, making this trip at the end of their lives. But there were other visitors in Bali and they were mostly young. They looked to Milly like innocent witches and princelings. They slept on the beach, cooked over fires, played guitars; she saw them strolling barefoot or eating mountains of food or lazing in the sand. There was not a sign of damage on them. She envied them their youth. For a week Milly swam in the hotel's pool, had a nap after lunch, took her first drink at six and went to bed early: it was like a spell of convalescence, and when she saw she had established this routine she was annoyed. One night, drinking in the bar, she was joined by an Australian. He talked about his children in the hurt remote way of a divorced man. At midnight, Milly stood up and snapped her handbag shut. The man said, "You're not going, are you?"

"I've paid for my share of the drinks," she said. "Was there something you wanted?"

But she knew, and she smiled at the fumbling man, almost pitying him.

"Perhaps I'll see you tomorrow," she said, and was gone.

She left the hotel, crossed by the pool to the beach, and walked toward a fire. It was the makeshift camp of the young people and there they sat, around the fire, singing. She hesitated to go near and she believed that she could not be seen standing in that darkness, listening to the music. But a voice said, "Hey! Come over here, stranger!"

She went over, and seating herself in the sand, saw the strumming boy. But her joining the group was not acknowledged. The youths sat crosslegged, like monks at prayer, facing the fire and the music. How many times, on a beach or by a roadside, had she seen groups like this and, almost alarmed, looked away! Even now she felt like an impostor. Someone might ask her age and laugh when she disclosed it. She wished she was not wearing such expensive slacks; she wished she looked like these people — and she hoped they would not remind her of her difference. She was glad for the dark.

Someone moved behind her. She started to rise, but he reached out and steadied her with his arm and hugged her. She relaxed and let him hold her. In the firelight she saw his face: twenty years old! She put her head against his shoulder and he adjusted his grip to hold her closer. And she trembled — for the first time since leaving Ayer Hitam — and wondered how she could stop herself from rolling him over on the sand and devouring him. Feeling that hunger, she grew afraid and said she had to go: she didn't want to startle the boy.

"I'll walk you back to the hotel," he said.

"I can find the way." Her voice was insistent; she didn't want to lose control.

The boy tagged along, she heard him trampling the sand; she wanted him to act — but how? Throw her down, fling off her clothes, make love to her? It was mad. Then it was too late, the hotel lights illuminated the beach; and she was relieved it had not happened. *I must be careful* — she almost spoke it.

"Will I see you again?"

"Perhaps," she said. She was on her own ground: the white hotel loomed behind the palms. Now — here — it was the boy who was the stranger.

"I want to sleep with you." It was not arrogant but imploring.

"Not now."

Not now. It should have been *no.* But marriage taught you how to be perfunctory, and Milly had, as a single woman, regained a lazy sense of hope. *No* was the prudent answer, *Not now* was what she had wanted to say — so she had said it. And the next day the boy was back, peering from the beach at Milly, who lounged by the pool. In the sunlight he looked even younger, with a shyness that might have been an effect of the sun's brightness, making him hunch and avert his eyes. He did not know where to begin, she saw that.

Milly waved to him. He signaled back and like an obedient pet responding to a mistress's nod came forward, vaulted the hibiscus hedge, smiling. Instead of taking the chair next to her he crouched at her feet, seeming to hide himself.

"They won't send you away," said Milly. "You can say you're my guest."

The boy shrugged. "At night — after everyone clears out — we come here swimming." He was silent, then he said, "Naked."

"How exciting," said Milly, frowning.

Seeing that it was mockery, the boy did not reply. He got to his feet. For a moment, Milly thought he was going to bound over the hedge and leave her. But in a series of athletic motions he strode to the edge of the pool, and without pausing tipped himself into it. He swam under water and Milly followed his blue shorts to the far end of the pool where he surfaced like a hound, gasping and tossing his head. He returned, swimming powerfully, flinging his arms into the water. But he did not climb out of the pool; he rested his forearms on the tiles and said, "Come in. I'll teach you how to swim."

"I was swimming before you were born." She wished she had not said it, she wished it was not true. She picked up a magazine from her lap and plucked at a page.

The boy was beside her, dripping.

"Take this," she said, and handed him a towel. He buried his face in it with an energy that aroused her, then he wiped his arms and threw it aside.

"Time for lunch," said Milly.

"Let me treat you," said the boy.

"That's very thoughtful of you," said Milly, "but I'm afraid they won't let you in the dining room like that."

"They have room service. We can have it sent up — eat on the balcony."

"You seem to be inviting yourself to my room," said Milly.

"No," said the boy, "I'm inviting you to mine."

Milly almost laughed. She said, *"Here?"*

"Sure. I've been here for about six weeks."

"I've never seen you at breakfast."

"I never eat breakfast," said the boy. "And I've only used my room a few times in the past week or so. I met a girl over on the beach — they have a house there. But my stuff is still in my room. My money, camera, passport, watch — the rest of it. I don't want it stolen."

"It must be fearfully expensive."

"My mother pays."

"How very American."

"She's on a tour — in Hong Kong," said the boy. "I thought we were talking about lunch."

"If you're a guest at this hotel, then you must have other clothes here. I suggest you dress properly, and if there's an empty chair at my table I have no objection to your joining me." Her voice, that fastidious tone, surprised and appalled her.

The boy's name was Mark. He told her that over lunch, but he said very little else. He was so young there was practically nothing he could say about himself beyond his name, and it was for Milly to keep the conversation going. It was not easy in her new voice. She described her trip through Indonesia, everything that had happened to her since leaving Ayer Hitam, but after that she was stumped. She would not speak about Lloyd or the divorce, and it angered her that it was impossible to speak about her life without discussing her marriage. Nearly twenty years had to be suppressed, and it seemed as if nothing had happened in those years that could matter to this young boy.

To his timid questions she said, "You wouldn't understand." She was hard on him. She knew why: she wanted him in the simplest way, and she resented wanting him. She objected to that desire in herself that would not allow her to go on alone. She did not want to look foolish — the age difference was ridicule enough — and wondered if in shrinking from an involvement she would reject him. She feared having him, she feared losing him. He told her he was nineteen and eagerly added the date of his next birthday.

Milly said, "Time for my nap."

"See you later, then," said Mark. He shook her hand.

In her room, she cursed herself. It had not occurred to her that he might not be interested. But perhaps this was so. He had a girl, one of the innocent witches; but her fate was the Australian who, late at night, rattled the change in his pocket and drawled for a persuasive way to interest her. She pulled the curtains, shutting out the hot sun, and for the first time since she arrived lay down on her bed wondering not if she should go, but where.

She closed her eyes and heard a knock on the door. She got out of bed, sighed, and opened the door a crack. "What is it?"

"Let me come in," said Mark. "Please."

She stared and said nothing. Then she moved aside and let the boy swing the door open. He did this with unnecessary force, as if he had expected her to resist.

Milly had not written any letters. A few postcards, a message about the weather. Letters were an effort because letters required either candor or wit, and her solitary existence had

hardened her to both. What Milly had done, almost since
the hour she had left Ayer Hitam, was rehearse conversations
with an imaginary friend, a woman, for whom in anecdote she
would describe the pleasures of divorce. Flying alone. The
looks you got in hotels. The Australian. A room of one's
own. The witches and princelings on the beach. Misunder-
standings. The suspicious eyes of other men's wives. The
mystery and the aroma of sexuality a single woman carried
past mute strangers.

Listen, she imagined herself saying; then she reported,
assessed, justified. It was a solitary traveler's habit, one en-
forced by her separation from Lloyd. She saw herself leaning
over a large menu, in the racket of a restaurant — flowers on
the table, two napkin cones, a dish of olives — and she heard
her own voice: *I think a nineteen-year-old boy and a woman
of — let's be frank — forty-one — I think they're perfectly
matched, sexually speaking. Yes, I really do. They're at some
kind of peak. That boy can have four or five orgasms in a row,
but so can a middle-aged woman — given the chance. It's the
middle-aged man with all his routines and apologies that
makes the woman feel inadequate. Sex for a boy, granted, is
usually a letdown because he's always trying himself out on a
girl his age, and what could be duller? It hurts, Jim, and hurry
up, and what if my parents find out? What I'm saying, and I
don't think it's anything to be ashamed of, is Mark and I were
well-matched, not in spite of our ages, but on the contrary, on
the contrary. It was like coaching a champion. I know I was
old enough to be his mother, but that's just the point. The
age ratio isn't insignificant. Don't laugh — the boy of a certain
age and his mother would make the best of lovers —*

But lovers was all they'd make. Conversation with Mark
was impossible. He would say, "I know a guy who has a
fantastic yacht in Baltimore."

A yacht. At the age of twenty-three, when Mark was one,

Milly had driven her own car to the south of France and stayed with her uncle, a famous lawyer. That handsome man had taken her on his yacht, poured her champagne, and tried to seduce her. He had failed, and angrily steered the yacht close to the rocky shore, to scare her. Later he bought her an expensive ring, and in London took her to wonderful restaurants, treating her like his mistress. He renamed his yacht *Milly*. Lloyd knew part of the story. To Mark Milly said, "I was on a yacht once, but I was much younger then."

For three weeks, in her room, in his, and twice on the beach, they made love. They kissed openly and made no secret of the affair. The guests at the hotel might whisper, but they never stayed longer than a few days, and they took their disapproval away with them. Milly herself wondered sometimes what would happen to her when Mark left, and she grew anxious when she remembered that she would have to leave eventually. She had no destination; she stayed another month: it was now November, and before Christmas she would exhaust herself of this boy. She was not calculating, but she saw nothing further for him. The affair, so complete on this bright island, would fail anywhere else.

Mark spoke of college, of books he planned to read, of jobs he'd like to have. It was all a hopeful itinerary she had traced before: she'd made that trip years ago, she'd read the books and known all the stops. She felt — listening to him telling her nothing new — as if she'd returned from a long sojourn in the world, one on which he, encumbered with ambition, was just setting out. She smiled at his innocent plans, and she gave him some encouragement; she would not disappoint him and tell him he would find nothing. He never asked for advice; he was too young to know the questions. She could tell him a great deal, but youth was ignorance in a splendid body: he wouldn't listen.

"I want to marry you," he said one day, and it sounded to

Milly like the expression of a longing that could never be fulfilled, like saying, *If only I could marry you!*

"I want to marry you, too," she said in the same way.

He kissed her and said, "We could do it here, the way the Balinese do — with a feast, music, dancing."

"I'll wear flowers in my hair."

"Right," he said. "We'll go up to Ubud and — "

"Oh, God," she said, "you're serious."

His face fell. He said, "Aren't you?"

"I've been married," she said, without enthusiasm, as she had once said to him, "I've been to Monte Carlo," implying that the action could not possibly be repeated.

"I've got lots of money," he said.

"Spend it wisely." It was the closest she had ever come to giving him advice.

"It would make things easier for us."

"This is as easy as it can ever be," she said. "Anyway, it's your mother's money, so stop talking this way. We can't get married and that's that."

"You don't have to marry me," he said. "Come to the States — we'll live together."

"And then what?"

"We'll drive around."

"What about your college — all those plans of yours?"

"They don't matter."

"Drive around!" She laughed hard at the thought of them in a car, speeding down a road, not stopping. Could anything short of marriage itself be a more boring exertion than that? He looked quite excited by the prospect of driving in circles.

"What's wrong?"

"I'm a bit old for that sort of thing."

"We can do anything you want — anything," he said. "Just live with me. No strings. Look, we can't stay here forever — "

It was true: she had nowhere to go. Milly was not fool enough to believe that it could work for any length of time, but for a month or two it might be fun. Then somewhere else, alone, to make a real start.

"We'll see," she said.

"Smile," he said.

She did and said, "What would you tell your mother?"

"I've already told her."

"*No!* What did she say?"

"She wants to meet you."

"Perhaps — one day." But the very thought of it filled her with horror.

"Soon," he said. "I wrote to her in Hong Kong. She replied from Bangkok. She'll be here in a week or so."

"Mine was so pathetic when I left him," Milly was saying. "I almost felt sorry for him. Now I can't stand the thought of him."

"As time goes on," said Maxine, "you'll hate him more and more." Abstractedly, she said, "I can't bear them to touch me."

"No," said Milly, "I don't think I could ever hate — "

Maxine laughed. "I just thought of it!"

"What?"

"The position my husband suggested. It was called 'The Autumn Dog.' Chinese, I think. You do it backward. It was impossible, of course — and grotesque, like animals in the bushes. He accused me of not trying — and guess what he said?"

"Backward!"

"He said, 'Max, it might save our marriage'!"

It struck Milly that there were only a few years — seconds in the life of the world — when that futile sentence had meaning. The years had coincided with her own marriage, but she had endured them and, like Maxine, earned her freedom. She had borne marriage long enough to see it disproved.

"But it didn't save it — it couldn't," said Maxine. Her face darkened. She said, "He was evil. He wanted Mark. But Mark wouldn't have him — he was devoted to me."

"Mark is a nice boy."

Maxine said, "Mark is lovely."

"At first I was sorry he told you about me. I was afraid to meet you. I though you'd dislike me."

"But you're not marrying him, are you?"

"I couldn't," said Milly. "Anyway, I'm through with marriage."

"Good," said Maxine. "The Autumn Dog."

"And Max," said Milly, using the woman's name for the first time, "I don't want you for a mother-in-law!"

"No — we'll be friends."

"What a pity I'm leaving here."

"Then we must leave together."

And the other woman's replies had come so quickly that Milly heard herself agreeing to a day, a flight, a destination.

"Poor Mark," said Milly at last.

"He's a lovely boy," said Maxine. "You have no idea. We go to plays together. He reads to me. I buy all his clothes. I like to be seen with him. Having a son like Mark is so much better than having a husband."

Milly felt the woman staring at her. She dropped her eyes.

"Or a friend like you," said Maxine. "That's much better. He told me all about you — he's very frank. He made me jealous, but that was silly, wasn't it? I think you're a very kind person."

She reached across the table. She took Milly's fingers and squeezed.

"If you're kind to me we'll be such good friends."

"Please stop!" Milly wanted to say. The other woman was hurting her hand with the pressure of her rings, and she seemed to smile at the panic on Milly's face. Finally, Milly said it, and another fear made the demand into a plea. Maxine relaxed her grip, but she held on, even after Mark appeared at the agreed time, to hear the verdict.

8. Dengué Fever

THERE IS a curious tree, native to Malaysia, called "The Midnight Horror." We had several in Ayer Hitam, one in an overgrown part of the Botanical Gardens, the other in the front garden of William Ladysmith's house. His house was huge, nearly as grand as mine, but I was the American Consul and Ladysmith was an English teacher on a short contract. I assumed it was the tree that had brought the value of his house down. The house itself had been built before the war — one of those great breezy places, a masterpiece of colonial carpentry, with cement walls two feet thick and window blinds the size of sails on a Chinese junk. It was said that it had been the center of operations during the occupation. All this history diminished by a tree! In fact, no local person would go near the house; the Chinese members of the staff at Ladysmith's school chose to live in that row of low warrens near the bus depot.

During the day the tree looked comic, a tall simple pole like an enormous coatrack, with big leaves that looked like branches — but there were very few of them. It was covered with knobs, stark black things; and around the base of the trunk there were always fragments of leaves that looked like shattered bones, but not human bones.

At night the tree was different, not comic at all. It was

Ladysmith who showed me the underlined passage in his copy of Professor Corner's *Wayside Trees of Malaya*. Below the entry for *Oroxylum indicum* it read, "Botanically, it is the sole representative of its kind; aesthetically, it is monstrous . . . The corolla begins to open about 10 P.M., when the tumid, wrinkled lips part and the harsh odour escapes from them. By midnight, the lurid mouth gapes widely and is filled with stink . . . The flowers are pollinated by bats which are attracted by the smell and, holding to the fleshy corolla with the claws on their wings, thrust their noses into its throat; scratches, as of bats, can be seen on the fallen leaves the next morning . . ."

Smelly! Ugly! Pollinated by bats! I said, "No wonder no one wants to live in this house."

"It suits me fine," said Ladysmith. He was a lanky fellow, very pleasant, one of our uncomplicated Americans who thrive in bush postings. He cycled around in his bermuda shorts, organizing talent shows in *kampongs*. His description in my consulate file was "Low risk, high gain." Full of enthusiasm and blue-eyed belief; and open-hearted: he was forever having tea with tradesmen, whose status was raised as soon as he crossed the threshold.

Ladysmith didn't come round to the Club much, although he was a member and had appeared in the Footlighters' production of Maugham's *The Letter*. I think he disapproved of us. He was young, one of the Vietnam generation with a punished conscience and muddled notions of colonialism. That war created dropouts, but Ladysmith I took to be one of the more constructive ones, a volunteer teacher. After the cease-fire there were fewer; now there are none, neither hippies nor do-gooders. Ladysmith was delighted to take his guilt to Malaysia, and he once told me that Ayer Hitam was more lively than his hometown, which surprised me until he said he was from Caribou, Maine.

He was tremendously popular with his students. He had put up a backboard and basketball hoop in the playground and after school he taught them the fundamentals of the game. He was, for all his apparent awkwardness, an athletic fellow, though it didn't show until he was in action — jumping or dribbling a ball down the court. Perhaps it never does. He ate like a horse, and knowing he lived alone I made a point of inviting him often to dinners for visiting firemen from Kuala Lumpur or Singapore. He didn't have a cook; he said he would not have a servant, but I don't believe he would have got any local person to live in his house, so close to that grotesque tree.

I was sorry but not surprised, two months after he arrived, to hear that Ladysmith had a fever. Ayer Hitam was malarial, and the tablets we took every Sunday like communion were only suppressants. The Chinese headmaster at the school stopped in at the Consulate and said that Ladysmith wanted to see me. I went that afternoon.

The house was empty; a few chairs in the sitting room, a shelf of paperbacks, a short-wave radio, and in the room beyond a table holding only a large bottle of ketchup. The kitchen smelled of peanut butter and stale bread. Bachelor's quarters. I climbed the stairs, but before I entered the bedroom I heard Ladysmith call out in an anxious voice, "Who is it?"

"Boy, am I glad to see you," he said, relaxing as I came through the door.

He looked thinner, his face was gray, his hair awry in bunches of standing hackles; and he lay in the rumpled bed as if he had been thrown there. His eyes were sunken and oddly colored with the yellow light of fever.

"Malaria?"

"I think so — I've been taking chloroquine. But it doesn't seem to be working. I've got the most awful headache." He closed his eyes. "I can't sleep. I have these nightmares. I —"

"What does the doctor say?"

"I'm treating myself," said Ladysmith.

"You'll kill yourself," I said. "I'll send Alec over tonight."

We talked for a while, and eventually I convinced Ladysmith that he needed attention. Alec Stewart was a club member Ladysmith particularly disliked. He wasn't a bad sort, but as he was married to a Chinese girl he felt he could call them "Chinks" without blame. He had been a ship's surgeon in the Royal Navy and had come to Ayer Hitam after the war. With a young wife and all that sunshine he was able to reclaim some of his youth. Back at the office I sent Peeraswami over with a pot of soup and the latest issue of *Newsweek* from the consulate library.

Alec went that night. I saw him at the Club later. He said, "Our friend's pretty rocky."

"I had malaria myself," I said. "It wasn't much fun."

Alex blew a cautionary snort. "He's not got malaria. He's got dengué."

"Are you sure?"

"All the symptoms are there."

"What did you give him for it?"

"The only thing there is worth a docken — aspirin."

"I suppose he'll have to sweat it out."

"He'll do that all right." Alec leaned over. "The lad's having hallucinations."

"I didn't know that was a symptom of dengué," I said.

"Dengué's a curse."

He described it to me. It is a virus, carried by a mosquito, and begins as a headache of such voltage that you tremble and can't stand or sit. You're knocked flat; your muscles ache, you're doubled-up with cramp and your temperature stays

over a hundred. Then your skin becomes paper-thin, sensitive
to the slightest touch — the weight of a sheet can cause pain.
And your hair falls out — not all of it, but enough to fill a
comb. These severe irritations produce another agony, a de-
pression so black the dengué sufferer continually sobs. All the
while your bones ache, as if every inch of you has been
smashed with a hammer. This sensation of bruising gives
dengué its colloquial name, "breakbone fever." I pitied
Ladysmith.

Although it was after eleven when Alec left the Club, I
went straight over to Ladysmith's house. I was walking up
the gravel drive when I heard the most ungodly shriek —
frightening in its intensity and full of alarm. I did not recognize it as Ladysmith's — indeed, it scarcely sounded human.
But it was coming from his room. It was so loud and
changed in pitch with such suddenness it might easily have
been two or three people screaming, or a dozen doomed cats.
The Midnight Horror tree was in full bloom and filled the
night with stink.

Ladysmith lay in bed whimpering. The magazine I'd sent
him was tossed against the wall, and the effect of disorder was
heightened by the overhead fan which was lifting and ruffling
the pages.

He was propped on one arm, but seeing me he sighed and
fell back. His face was slick with perspiration and tear-streaks.
He was short of breath.

"Are you all right?"

"My skin is burning," he said. I noticed his lips were
swollen and cracked with fever, and I saw then how dengué
was like a species of grief.

"I thought I heard a scream," I said. Screaming takes
energy; Ladysmith was beyond screaming, I thought.

"Massacre," he said. "Soldiers — killing women and children. Horrible. Over there — " He pointed to a perfectly ordinary table with a jug of water on it, and he breathed, "War. You should see their faces, all covered with blood. Some have arms missing. I've never — " He broke off and began to sob.

"Alec says you have dengué fever," I said.

"Two of them — women. They look the same," said Ladysmith, lifting his head. "They scream at me, and it's so loud! They have no teeth!"

"Are you taking the aspirin?" I saw the amber jar was full.

"Aspirin! For this!" He lay quietly, then said, "I'll be all right. Sometimes it's nothing — just a high temperature. Then these Chinese . . . then I get these dreams."

"About war?"

"Yes. Flashes."

As gently as I could I said, "You didn't want to go to Vietnam, did you?"

"No. Nobody wanted to go. I registered as a C.O."

Hallucinations are replies. Peeraswami was always seeing Tamil ghosts on his way home. They leaped from those green fountains by the road the Malays call *daun pontianak* — "ghost leaf" — surprising him with plates of hot samosas or tureens of curry; not so much ghosts as ghostesses. I told him to eat something before setting out from home in the dark and he stopped seeing them. I took Ladysmith's visions of massacre to be replies to his conscientious objection. It is the draft-dodger who speaks most graphically of war, not the soldier. Pacifists know all the atrocity stories.

But Ladysmith's hallucinations had odd highlights: the soldiers he saw weren't American. They were dark orientals in dirty undershirts, probably Vietcong, and mingled with the screams of the people with bloody faces was another sound, the creaking of bicycle seats. So there were two horrors — the massacre and these phantom cyclists. He was especially frightened by the two women with no teeth, who opened their mouths wide and screamed at him.

I said, "Give it a few days."

"I don't think I can take much more of this."

"Listen," I said. "Dengué can depress you. You'll feel like giving up and going home — you might feel like hanging yourself. But take these aspirin and keep telling yourself — whenever you get these nightmares — it's dengué fever."

"No teeth, and their guns are dripping with blood — "

His head dropped to the pillow, his eyes closed, and I remember thinking: everyone is fighting this war, everyone in the world. Poor Ladysmith was fighting hardest of all. Lying there he could have been bivouacked in the Central Highlands, haggard from a siege, his dengué a version of battle fatigue.

I left him sleeping and walked again through the echoing house. But the smell had penetrated to the house itself, the high thick stink of rotting corpses. It stung my eyes and I almost fainted with the force of it until, against the moon, I saw that blossoming coatrack and the wheeling bats — The Midnight Horror.

"Rotting flesh," Ladysmith said late the next afternoon. I tried not to smile. I had brought Alec along for a second look. Ladysmith began describing the smell, the mutilated people, the sound of bicycles, and those Chinese women, the toothless ones. The victims had pleaded with him. Ladysmith looked wretched.

Alec said, "How's your head?"

"It feels like it's going to explode."

Alec nodded. "Joints a bit stiff?"

"I can't move."

"Dengué's a curse." Alec smiled: doctors so often do when their grim diagnosis is proved right.

"*I can't* — " Ladysmith started, then grimaced and continued in a softer tone. "I can't sleep. If I could only sleep I'd be all right. For God's sake give me something to make me sleep."

Alec considered this.

"Can't you give him anything?" I asked.

"I've never prescribed a sleeping pill in my life," said Alec, "and I'm not going to do so now. Young man, take my advice. Drink lots of liquid — you're dehydrating. You've got a severe fever. Don't underestimate it. It can be a killer. But I guarantee if you follow my instructions, get lots of bed rest, take aspirin every four hours, you'll be right as ninepence."

"My hair is falling out."

Alex smiled — right again. "Dengué," he said. "But you've still got plenty. When you've as little hair as I have you'll have something to complain about."

Outside the house I said, "That tree is the most malignant thing I've ever seen."

Alec said, "You're talking like a Chink."

"Sure, it looks innocent enough now, with the sun shining on it. But have you smelled it at night?"

"I agree. A wee aromatic. Like a Bengali's fart."

"If we cut it down I think Ladysmith would stop having his nightmares."

"Don't be a fool. That tree's medicinal. The Malays use it for potions. It works — I use it myself."

"Well, if it's so harmless why don't the Malays want to live in this house?"

"It's not been offered to a Malay. How many Malay

teachers do you know? It's the Chinks won't live here — I don't have a clue why that's so, but I won't have you running down that tree. It's going to cure our friend."

I stopped walking. "What do you mean by that?"

Alec said, "The aspirin — or rather, not the aspirin. I'm using native medicine. Those tablets are made from the bark of that tree — I wish it didn't have that shocking name."

"You're giving him *that?*"

"Calm down, it'll do him a world of good," Alex said brightly. "Ask any witch doctor."

I slept badly myself that night, thinking of Alec's ridiculous cure — he had truly gone bush — but I was tied up all day with visa inquiries and it was not until the following evening that I got back to Ladysmith's. I was determined to take him away. I had aspirin at my house; I'd keep him away from Alec.

Downstairs, I called out and knocked as usual to warn him I'd come, and as usual there was no response from him. I entered the bedroom and saw him asleep, but uncovered. Perhaps the fever had passed: his face was dry. He did not look well, but then few people do when they're sound asleep — most take on the ghastly color of illness. Then I saw that the amber bottle was empty — the "aspirin" bottle.

I tried to feel his pulse. Impossible: I've never been able to feel a person's pulse, but his hand was cool, almost cold. I put my ear against his mouth and thought I could detect a faint purr of respiration.

It was dusk when I arrived, but darkness in Ayer Hitam fell quickly, the blanket of night dropped and the only warning was the sound of insects tuning up, the chirrup of geckoes and those squeaking bats making for the tree. I switched on the lamp and as I did so heard a low cry, as of someone dying

in dreadful pain. And there by the window — just as Ladysmith had described — I saw the moonlit faces of two Chinese women, smeared with blood. They opened their mouths
and howled; they were toothless and their screeches seemed
to gain volume from that emptiness.

"Stop!" I shouted.

The two faces in those black rags hung there, and I caught
the whiff of the tree which was the whiff of wounds. It
should have scared me, but it only surprised me. Ladysmith
had prepared me, and I felt certain that he had passed that
horror on. I stepped forward, caught the cord, and dropped
the window blinds. The two faces were gone.

This took seconds, but an after-image remained, like a lamp
switched rapidly on and off. I gathered up Ladysmith. Having
lost weight he was very light, pathetically so. I carried him
downstairs and through the garden to the road.

Behind me, in the darkness, was the rattle of pedals, the
squeak of a bicycle seat. The phantom cyclists! It gave me a
shock, and I tried to run, but carrying Ladysmith I could not
move quickly. The cycling noises approached, frantic squeak-
ings at my back. I spun round.

It was a trishaw, cruising for fares. I put Ladysmith on the
seat, and running alongside it we made our way to the mission
hospital.

A stomach pump is little more than a slender rubber tube
pushed into one nostril and down the back of the throat. A
primitive device: I couldn't watch. I stayed until Ladysmith
regained consciousness. But it was useless to talk to him. His
stomach was empty and he was coughing up bile, spewing
into a bucket. I told the nursing sister to keep an eye on
him.

I said, "He's got dengué."

The succeeding days showed such an improvement in

Ladysmith that the doctors insisted he be discharged to make room for more serious cases. And indeed everyone said he'd made a rapid recovery. Alec was astonished, but told him rather sternly, "You should be ashamed of yourself for taking that overdose."

Ladysmith was well, but I didn't have the heart to send him back to that empty house. I put him up at my place. Normally, I hated houseguests — they interfered with my reading and never seemed to have much to do themselves except punish my gin bottle. But Ladysmith was unobtrusive. He drank milk, he wrote letters home. He made no mention of his hallucinations, and I didn't tell him what I'd thought I'd seen. In my own case I believe his suggestions had been so strong that I had imagined what he had seen — somehow shared his own terror of the toothless women.

One day at lunch Ladysmith said, "How about eating out tonight? On me. A little celebration. After all, you saved my life."

"Do you feel well enough to face the club buffet?"

He made a face. "I hate the Club — no offense. But I was thinking of a meal in town. What about that *kedai* — City Bar? I had a terrific meal there the week I arrived. I've been meaning to go back."

"You're the boss."

It was a hot night. The verandah tables were taken, so we had to sit inside, jammed against a wall. We ordered *mee-hoon* soup, spring rolls, pork strips, fried *kway-teow*, and a bowl of *laksa* that seemed to blister the lining of my mouth.

"One thing's for sure," said Ladysmith, "I won't get dengué fever again for a while. The sister said I'm immune for a year."

"Thank God for that," I said. "By then you'll be back in Caribou, Maine."

"I don't know," he said. "I like it here."

He was smiling, glancing around the room, poking noodles into his mouth. Then I saw him lose control of his chopsticks. His jaw dropped, he turned pale, and I thought for a moment that he was going to cry.

"Is anything wrong?"

He shook his head, but he looked stricken.

"It's this food," I said. "You shouldn't be eating such strong — "

"No," he said. "It's those pictures."

On the whitewashed wall of the *kedai* was a series of framed photographs, old hand-colored ones, lozenge-shaped, like huge lockets. Two women and some children. Not so unusual; the Chinese always have photographs of relations around — a casual reverence. One could hardly call them a pious people; their brand of religion is ancestor worship, the simple display of the family album. But I had not realized until then that Woo Boh Swee's relations had had money. The evidence was in the pictures: both women were smiling, showing large sets of gold dentures.

"That's them," said Ladysmith.

"Who?" I said. Staring at them I noticed certain wrinkles of familiarity, but the Chinese are very hard to tell apart. The cliché is annoyingly true.

Ladysmith put his chopsticks down and began to whisper: "The women in my room — that's *them*. That one had blood on her hair, and the other one — "

"Dengué fever," I said. "You said they didn't have any teeth. Now I ask you — look at those teeth. You've got the wrong ladies, my boy."

"No!"

His pallor had returned, and the face I saw across the table was the one I had seen on that pillow. I felt sorry for him, and as helpless as I had before.

Woo Boh Swee, the owner of City Bar, went by the table. He was brisk, snapping a towel. "Okay? Anything? More beer? What you want?"

"We're fine, Mr. Woo," I said. "But I wonder if you can tell us something. We were wondering who those women are in the pictures — over there."

He looked at the wall, grunted, lowered his head, and simply walked away, muttering.

"I don't get it," I said. I left the table and went to the back of the bar, where Boh Swee's son Reggie — the "English" son — was playing mahjong. I asked Reggie the same question: who are they?

"I'm glad you asked me," said Reggie. "Don't mention them to my father. One's his auntie, the other one's his sister. It's a sad story. They were cut up during the war by the dwarf bandits. That's what my old man calls them in Hokkien. The Japanese. It happened over at the headquarters — what they used for headquarters when they occupied the town. My old man was in Singapore."

"But the Japanese were only here for a few months," I said.

"Bunch of thieves," said Reggie. "They took anything they could lay their hands on. They used those old ladies for housegirls, at the headquarters, that big house, where the tree is. Then they killed them, just like that, and hid the bodies — we never found the graves. But that was before they captured Singapore. The British couldn't stop them, you know. The dwarf bandits were clever — they pretended they were Chinese and rode all the way to the Causeway on bicycles."

I looked back at the table. Ladysmith was staring, his eyes again bright with fever, staring at those gold teeth.

9. The South Malaysia Pineapple Growers' Association

THEY HAD a drama society, but it was not called the South Malaysia Pineapple Growers' Drama Society; it was the Footlighters, it met on Wednesday evenings in the club lounge, and the official patron was the Sultan. He seldom came to the plays and never to the Club. It was just as well, the Footlighters said; when the Sultan was at the theater you couldn't drink at the bar between the acts, which was why most of the audience came, the men anyway. Angela Miller, who drove down from Layang Layang every Wednesday, said the Sultan was a frightful old bore whose single interest was polo.

An effortlessly deep-voiced woman, much more handsome at forty-five than she had been pretty at twenty, Angela had played a Wilde heroine six years before — that was in Kota Bharu — and found the role so agreeable, so suited to her temper, that in moments of stress she became that heroine; telling a story, she used the heroine's inflections and certain facial expressions, especially incredulity. Often it allowed her to manage her anger.

It was Angela who told the story of Jan's first visit to the Club. Jan had looked at the photographs on the wall of the bar and then sat in a lounge chair sipping her gimlet while the other members talked. Only Angela had seen Jan rush to the window and exclaim, "What a *lovely* time of day!"

"All I could see were the tennis courts," said Angela later, "but little Jan said, 'Look at the air — it's like *silk*.' "

Jan Prosser was new, not only to the Club and the Foot-lighters, but to Ayer Hitam, where her husband, Rupert, had just been posted to cut down a rubber estate and oversee the planting of oil palms.

"Anyone," said Angela, "who spends that long looking out the window *has* to be new to Ayer Hitam. I look out the window and don't see a blessed thing!"

It had happened only the previous week. Already it was one of Angela's stories; she had a story to explain the behavior of every Footlighter and, it was said, most planter families. That exclamation at sundown was all the Footlighters knew of Jan on the evening they met to pick a new play. She was a pale girl, perhaps twenty-six, with a small head and damp nervous eyes. Some of the male Footlighters had spoken to Jan's husband; they had found him hearty, with possibilities backstage, but mainly interested in fishing.

Angela was chairing the meeting; they had narrowed the selection to *Private Lives* and *The World of Suzie Wong*, and before anyone asked her opinion, Jan said, "We did *Private Lives* in Nigeria." It was an innocent remark, but Jan was slightly impatient and gave it a dogmatic edge, which surprised the rest into silence.

"Oh, really?" said Angela in her intimating bass after a pause. She trilled the *r* as she would have done on stage, and she glared at Jan.

"Yes, um," said Jan, "I played Amanda. Rupert helped with the sets." She smiled and closed her eyes, remembering. "What a night that was. It rained absolute *buckets*."

"Maybe we should put it on here," said Duff Gillespie. "We need some rain over at my place."

Everyone laughed, Angela loudest of all, and Jan said, "It's a very witty play. Two excellent women's parts and lots of good lines."

"Epicene," said Tony Evans.

"I've noticed," said Henry Eliot, a white-haired man who usually played fathers, "that when you use a big word, Tony, you never put it in a sentence. It's rather cowardly."

"That's who we're talking about," said Tony, affecting rather than speaking in the Welsh accent that was natural to him. "Noel Coward."

"Too-bloody-shay," said Duff, "pardon my French."

Jan looked from face to face; she wondered if they were making fun of her.

"That settles it," said Angela. "*Suzie Wong* it is."

"When did we decide that?" asked Henry, making a face.

"You didn't," said Angela, "*I* did. We can't have squabbling." She smiled at Jan. "You'll find me fantastically dictatorial, my dear. Pass me that script, would you, darling?" Angela took the gray booklet that Tony Evans had been flipping through. She put it on the table, opened it decisively to *Cast, in Order of Their Appearance,* and ran the heel of her hand down the fold, flattening it. She said, "Now for the cast."

At eleven-thirty, all the main parts had been allotted. "Except one," said Jan.

"I beg your pardon," said Angela.

"I mean, it's all set, isn't it? Except that we haven't — " She looked at the others " — we haven't decided the biggest part, have we?"

Angela gave Jan her look of incredulity. She did it with wintry slowness, and it made Jan pause and know she had said something wrong. So Jan laughed, it was a nervous laugh, and she said, "I mean, who's Suzie?"

"Who indeed?" said Henry in an Irish brogue. He took his pipe out of his mouth to chuckle; then he returned the pipe and the chuckling stopped. He derived an unusual joy from watching two women disagree. His smile showed triumph.

"You've got your part," said Angela, losing control of her accent. "I should say it's a jolly good one."

"Oh, I know that!" Jan said. "But I was wondering about — " She looked at the table and said, "I take it you're going to play Suzie."

"Unless anyone has any serious objections," said Angela. No one said a word. Angela addressed her question to Jan, "Do you have any serious objections?"

"Well, not *serious* objections," said Jan, trying to sound good-humored.

"Maybe she thinks — " Duff started.

Angela interrupted, "Perhaps I'm too old for the part, Jan, is that what you're trying to say?"

"God, not that," said Jan, becoming discomposed. "Honestly Angela, I think you're perfect for it, really I do."

"What is it then?"

Jan seemed reluctant to begin, but she had gone too far to withdraw. Her hands were clasped in her lap and now she was speaking to Duff, whose face was the most sympathetic. "I don't want to make this sound like an objection, but the point is, Suzie is supposed to be, well, *Chinese* . . . and, Angela, you're not, um, Chinese. Are you?"

"Not as far as I know," said Angela, raising a laugh. The laughter subsided. "But I am an actress."

"I know that," said Jan, "and I'm dead sure you'd do a marvelous Suzie." Jan became eager. "I'm terribly excited about this production, really I am. But what if we got a Chinese girl from town to play Suzie. I mean, a *real* Chinese girl, with one of those dresses slit up the side and that long black hair and that sort of slinky — "

Angela's glare prevented Jan from going any further.

"It's a challenging role," said Angela, switching her expression from one of disapproval to one of profound interest. "But so are they all, and we must be up to it. Henry is going to play the old Chinese man. Would you prefer that Stanley did it?"

Stanley Chee, a man of sixty, with gold-rimmed glasses and a starched uniform, was Head Boy of the Club, and at that moment he could be seen — all heads turned — through the bar door, looking furtive as he wiped a bottle.

Jan shook her head from side to side.

"It's going to be a hard grind," said Angela, and she smiled. "But that's what acting is. Being someone else. Completely. That's what I tell all the new people."

10. The Butterfly of the Laruts

THE PEOPLE in Ayer Hitam stopped referring to her as Dr. Smith as soon as they set eyes on her. She was "that woman," then "our friend," and only much later, after she had left the district and when the legend was firmly established, was she Dr. Smith again, the title giving her name a greater mockery than anyone there could manage in a tone of voice. She didn't have much luck with her simple name; as everyone knew, even the man she married could not pronounce it. But that was not surprising: a narrow ornament, a sliver of ivory he wore in his lower lip, prevented him from saying most words clearly.

She flitted into town that first day in a bright, wax-print sarong, and with a loose pale blouse through which you could see her breasts in nodding motion. She might have been one of those ravished American women, grazing the parapet of middle age, with a monotonous libido and an expensive camera, vowing to have a fling at the romance travel was supposed to provide. But she was far from frivolous, and she had not been in the district long before it became apparent that she was anything but typical.

A typical visitor stayed at the Government Rest House or the Club, but Dr. Smith never went near either of them, nor did she stay at the Chinese hotels. Her few days in Ayer Hitam were passed at a Malay *kedai*, a flyblown shop on a back road. It was assumed she shared a room. You can imagine the speculation. But she had the magic travelers sometimes have, of finding in a place something the residents have missed and giving it a brief celebrity.

So, after she had gone into the jungle, some of us used this *kedai* and we discovered that it employed as sweepers several men from a small tribe of *orang asli* who lived sixty miles to the north, in an isolated pouch of jungle near one of Fred Squibb's timber estates. Their looks were unmistakable. That should have been our first clue: we knew she was an anthropologist, we heard she had taken a taxi north, and Squibb, the timber merchant, said the taxi had dropped her at the bush track which met the main road and extended some fifteen miles to the *kampong*. There had been, he said, half a dozen tribesmen — Laruts, they were called — squatting at the trampled mouth of the path. Squibb said they were waiting for her and that they might have been there, roosting like owls, for days.

We had seen anthropologists before. Their sturdy new clothes and neatly packed rucksacks, tape recorders and parcels of books and paper, gave them away immediately. But Dr. Smith caused a local sensation. No one since Sir Hugh Clifford had studied the Laruts; they were true natives, small people with compressed negroid features, clumsy innocent faces, and long arms, who had been driven into the interior as the Malays and Chinese crowded the peninsula. There were few in the towns. You saw them unexpectedly tucked in the bends of bush roads, with the merchandise they habitually sold — red and yellow parrots, flapping things snared in the jungle, unused to the ingeniously woven Larut cages; and orchids harvested from the trunks of forest trees; and butterflies, as large as those orchids, mounted lopsidedly in cigar boxes. The Laruts were our savages, proof we were civilized: Malays especially measured themselves by them. Their movements, jinking in the forest, were like the flights of the butterflies they sold on the roadsides with aboriginal patience. Selling such graceful stuff was appropriate to this gentle tribe, for as was well known, they were nonviolent: they did not make weapons, they didn't fight. They had been hunted for sport, like frail deer, by early settlers. As the Malays and the Chinese grew more quarrelsome and assertive, the Laruts responded by moving further and further inland, until they came to rest on hillsides and in swamps, enduring the extremes of landscape to avoid hostile contact.

Bur Dr. Smith found them, and a week later there were no Laruts on the road, no butterflies for sale, only the worn patches on the grassy verge where they had once waited with their cages and boxes, smoking their oddly shaped clay pipes.

At the Club, Angela said, "I expect we'll see her in town buying clothes." But no one saw her, nor did we see much of the Laruts. They had withdrawn, it seemed, to the deepest part of the forest, and their absence from the roads made those stretches particularly cheerless. We guessed at what might be going on in the Larut *kampong*, and with repetition our guesses acquired all the neatness and authority of facts. Then we had a witness.

Squibb went to the area; he brought back this story. He had borrowed a motorbike at one of his substations and had ridden it over the bush track until at last he came to the outskirts of the *kampong*. He saw some children playing and asked them in Malay if "the white queen" was around. They took him to her, and he said he was astonished to see her kneeling in the dust by a hut, pounding some food in a mortar with several Larut women. They were stripped to the waist and chanting.

"You could have knocked me over with a feather," Squibb said. He spat in disgust and went on to say how dirty she was; her sarong was in tatters, her hands filthy. Apparently he went over to her, but she ignored him. Finally, she spoke.

"Can't you see I'm busy?" She went on heaving the pestle.

Squibb was persistent. She said (and this was the sentence I heard Squibb repeating in the club lounge for days afterward): "We don't want you here."

There were other stories, but most of them seemed to originate with Squibb: the Ministry of Tourism was angry that the Laruts had stopped selling butterflies on the road; the missionaries in the area, Catholic fathers from Canada, were livid because the Larut children had stopped going to the mission school, and for the first time in many years the mission's dispensary — previously filled with snakebite victims and Laruts with appendicitis and strangulated hernias — was nearly empty. There was more: the Laruts had started to move their *kampong*, putting up huts in the heavily forested portion of jungle that adjoined Squibb's timber estate.

"She's a menace," Squibb said.

He came to me at the Consulate and sat, refusing to leave until I listened to the last of his stories.

"There's nothing I can do," I said.

"She's an American — you can send her home."

"I don't see any evidence of treachery here," I said.

"She's sticking her nose in where she's not wanted!"

"That's a matter for the Malaysians to decide."

"They're as browned-off as I am," Squibb said. He became solicitous about the Laruts; odd — he had always spoken of them as a nuisance, interrupting the smooth operation of his lumber mills with their poaching and thieving.

A day or two later, the District Commissioner dropped in. He was a dapper, soft-spoken Malay named Azhari, educated in London; he had a reputation as a sport, and his adventures with various women at the Club were well known. There were "Azhari stories." He informed me politely that he was serving a deportation order on Dr. Smith.

"What for?"

"Interfering in the internal affairs of our country," he said. I wondered if she had turned him down.

"You've been talking to Squibb," I said. He smiled; he didn't deny it.

It was Azhari's assistant who cycled to the village with the deportation order; it was he who brought us the news of the marriage.

At the Club, people said to me, "You Americans," and this was the only time in all my years at the Consulate there that Ayer Hitam was ever mentioned in the world's press. It was so unusual, seeing the town in the paper, mentions of the Club, City Bar, the *kedai* where Dr. Smith had stayed, each one shabbily hallowed to a shrine by the coarse prose of journalists. They attempted a description of our heat, our trees, our roads, our way of life; struggling to make us unique they only succeeded in making us ridiculous (I was the "youthful American Consul"). They spelled all our names wrong.

There were photographs of Dr. Smith and the chief. She wore a printed scarf across her breasts in a makeshift halter, her hair knotted, and around her neck a great wooden necklace. He had headgear of parrot feathers, leather armlets on his biceps, and heavy earrings; he was a small man of perhaps fifty, with a worried furrowed face and tiny ears. In the photographs he looked cross-eyed, but that might have been his worry distorted in the strong light. She towered over him, triumphant, wistful. His arm was awkwardly crooked in hers. Around them were many blurred grinning faces of Larut well-wishers.

"We are very much in love," she was reported to have said. "We plan to have lots of children. I know my duties as a Larut wife."

It was not simple. The Laruts, idle and good-hearted, were polygamous. The chief had eight wives. Dr. Smith was the ninth.

This was the last we heard of her for several months.

Father Lefever from the mission came to see me one afternoon. He was circumspect; he asked permission to smoke and then set fire to a stinking cheroot. In the middle of casual remarks about the late monsoon he said, "You must do something about that woman."

"So what Squibb said about the dispensary is true."

"I don't know what he said, but I think this woman could do a great deal of harm. The Laruts are a simple people — like children. They are not used to this attention."

"I haven't heard anything lately, though Squibb said they're treating themselves with native medicine — they've stopped coming to your dispensary."

The priest looked down. "And to church."

"That's their choice, one would guess."

"No, it's her. I know it. Not the Laruts."

"But *she's* a Larut," I said.

Azhari was firmer. He came demanding information on her background, by which he meant her past. I guessed his motive to be resentment: a man he regarded as a savage had become his sexual competitor. But the whole affair was beginning to annoy me. I told him it was none of my business, her marriage had given her Malaysian citizenship, and as far as I was concerned she was no longer an American subject. I said, "I don't see what all the fuss is about."

"You don't know these chaps," said Azhari. "They are special people in this country. They don't pay taxes, they don't vote, they can go anywhere they wish. And since that woman came there's been a lot of loose talk."

"Of what sort?"

"She's stirring them up," he said. But he didn't elaborate. "If you won't help me I'll go over your head to the Ambassador."

"Nothing would please me more."

All this interest in the Laruts, who until then had only sold butterflies, and were famous because they did not use violence.

Late one night, there was a loud rapping at the front door. Ah Wing answered it and seeing the visitors, said *"Sakais,"* with undisguised contempt.

A boy and an old man, obviously the chief. They came in and sat on the floor, the old man quite close, the boy — who was about twelve or thirteen — some distance away. They must have walked all the way from the village; their legs were wet and they had bits of broken leaf in their hair. They had brought the smell of the jungle into the room. The chief looked troubled; he nodded to the boy.

The boy said, "He wants you to take her away."

"His wife?" The boy jerked his head forward. "I can't do that. Only he can do that. Tell him he is her husband."

This was translated. The old man winced, and the scars beside his eyes bunched to tiny florets. He said something quickly, a signaling grunt. They had rehearsed this.

"He has money," the boy said. "He will pay you."

"Money doesn't matter," I said. I felt sorry for the old man: what had happened? Bullying, I imagined, threats of violence from Dr. Smith; what pacifist tribe could contain an American academic, a woman with a camera? I said, "There's a way. It's very simple — but he must be absolutely sure he never wants to see her again."

"He is sure." The boy didn't bother to translate. He knew his orders. He listened to what I said.

And it was so strange, the boy translating into the Larut language the process of divorce, the old man shaking his head, and the word for which there could not have been a Larut equivalent, recurring in the explanation as *vuss . . . vuss*. The old chief looked slightly shocked, and I was embarrassed; he was having this new glimpse of us, a revelation of a private cruelty of ours, a secret ritual that was available to him. At the end he wanted to give me money. I told him to save it for the lawyer.

The newspapers were interested; there was another influx of journalists from Singapore, but Dr. Smith left as soon as the chief engaged a lawyer, and this time she didn't pass through Ayer Hitam. The journalists caught up with her in Tokyo — or was it Los Angeles? I forget. The pity of it was that they took no notice of what followed, the Laruts' new village (and prosperity for the chief) in the remotest part of the state, the closing of the mission, and Squibb's timber operation, which, it was said, made that little bush track into a road wide enough for huge timber trucks to collect the trees that were felled in and around the derelict village.

11. The Tennis Court

EVERYONE HATED Shimura; but no one really knew him: Shimura was Japanese. He was not a member of the Club. About every two weeks he would stop one night in Ayer Hitam on his way to Singapore. He spent the day in Singapore and stopped again on the way back. Using us — which was how Evans put it — he was avoiding two nights at an expensive hotel. I say he wasn't in our club; yet he had full use of the facilities, because he was a member of the Selangor Club in Kuala Lumpur and we had reciprocal privileges. Seeing his blue Toyota appear in the driveway, Evans always said, "Here comes the freeloader."

Squibb said, "I say, there's a nip in the air."

And Alec said, "Shoot him down."

I didn't join them in their bigoted litany. I liked Shimura. I was ashamed of myself for not actively defending him, but I was sure he didn't need my help.

That year there were hundreds of Japanese businessmen in Kuala Lumpur selling transistor radios to the Malays. It seemed a harmless enough activity, but the English resented them and saw them as poaching on what they considered an exclusively British preserve. Evans said, "I didn't fight the war so that those people could tell us how to run our club."

Shimura was a tennis player. On his fifth or sixth visit he had suggested, in a way his stuttering English had blunted into a tactless complaint, that the ball-boys moved around too much.

"They must stand quiet."

It was the only thing he had ever said, and it damned him. Typical Japanese attitude, people said, treating our ball-boys like prisoners of war. Tony Evans, chairman of the tennis committee, found it unforgivable. He said to Shimura, "There are courts in Singapore," but Shimura only laughed.

He seemed not to notice that he was hated. His composure was perfect. He was a small dark man, fairly young, with ropes of muscle knotted on his arms and legs, and his crouch on the court made him seem four-legged. He played a hard darting game with a towel wound around his neck like a scarf; he barked loudly when he hit the ball.

He always arrived late in the afternoon, and before dinner played several sets with anyone who happened to be around. Alec had played him, so had Eliot and Strang; he had won every match. Evans, the best player in the Club, refused to meet him on the tennis court. If there was no one to play, Shimura hit balls against the wooden backboard, barking at the hard ones, and he practiced with such determination you could hear his grunts as far as the reading room. He ate alone and went to bed early. He spoke to no one; he didn't drink. I sometimes used to think that if he had spent some time in the bar, like the other temporary members who passed through Ayer Hitam, Shimura would have no difficulty.

Alec said, "Not very clubbable."

"Ten to one he's fiddling his expenses," said Squibb.

Evans criticized his lob.

He could not have been hated more. His nationality, his size, his stinginess, his laugh, his choice of tennis partners (once he had played Eliot's sexually browsing wife)—everything told against him. He was aloof, one of the worst social crimes in Malaysia; he was identified as a parasite, and worst of all he seemed to hold everyone in contempt. Offenses were invented: he bullied the ball-boys, he parked his car the wrong way, he made noises when he ate.

It may be hard to be an American — I sometimes thought so when I remembered our beleaguered Peace Corps teachers — but I believe it was even harder to be a Japanese in that place. They had lost the war and gained the world; they were unreadable, impossible to know; more courtly than the Chinese, they used this courtliness to conceal. The Chinese were secretive bumblers and their silences could be hysterical; the Japanese gave nothing away; they never betrayed their frenzy. This contempt they were supposed to have: it wasn't contempt, it was a total absence of trust in anyone who was not Japanese. And what was perhaps more to the point, they were the opposite to the English in every way I could name.

The war did not destroy the English — it fixed them in fatal attitudes. The Japanese were destroyed and out of that destruction came different men; only the loyalties were old — the rest was new. Shimura, who could not have been much more than thirty, was one of these new men, a postwar instrument, the perfectly calibrated Japanese. In spite of what everyone said, Shimura was an excellent tennis player.

So was Evans, and it was he who organized the club game: How to get rid of Shimura?

Squibb had a sentimental tolerance for Malays and a grudging respect for the Chinese, but like the rest of the club members he had an absolute loathing for the Japanese. When Alec said, "I suppose we could always debag him," Squibb replied fiercely, "I'd like to stick a *kukri* in his guts."

"We could get him for an infraction," said Strang.

"That's the trouble with the obnoxious little sod," said Squibb. "He doesn't break the rules. We're lumbered with him for life."

The hatred was old. The word "Changi" was associated with Shimura. Changi was the jail in Singapore where the British were imprisoned during the war, after the fall of the city, and Shimura was held personally responsible for what had gone on there: the water torture, the *rotan* floggings, the bamboo rack, the starvation and casual violence the Japanese inflicted on people they despised because they had surrendered.

"I know what we ought to do," said Alec. "He wants his tennis. We won't give him his tennis. If we kept him off the courts we'd never see his face here again."

"That's a rather low trick," said Evans.

"Have you got a better one?" said Squibb.

"Yes," said Evans. "Play him."

"I wouldn't play him for anything," said Squibb.

"He'd beat you in any case," said Alec.

Squibb said, "But he wouldn't beat Tony."

"Not me — I'm not playing him. I suggest we get someone else to beat him," said Evans. "These Japs can't stand humiliation. If he was really beaten badly we'd be well rid of him."

I said, "This is despicable. You don't know Shimura — you have no reason to dislike that man. I want no part of this."

"Then bugger off!" shouted Squibb, turning his red face on me. "We don't need a bloody Yank to tell us — "

"Calm yourself," said Alec. "There's ladies in the bar."

"Listen," I said to Squibb, "I'm a member of this Club. I'm staying right here."

"What about Shimura?" said Alec.

"It's just as I say, if he was beaten badly he'd be humiliated," said Evans.

Squibb was looking at me as he said, "There are some little fuckers you can't humiliate."

But Evans was smiling.

The following week Shimura showed up late one afternoon, full of beans. He changed, had tea alone, and then appeared on the court with the towel around his neck and holding his racket like a sword. He chopped the air with it and looked around for a partner.

The court was still except for Shimura's busy shadow, and at the far end two ball-boys crouched with their sarongs folded between their knees. Shimura hit a few practice shots on the backboard.

We watched him from the rear verandah, sitting well back from the railing: Evans, Strang, Alec, Squibb, and myself. Shimura glanced up and bounced the racket against his palm. A ball-boy stood and yawned and drew out a battered racket. He walked toward Shimura, and though Shimura could not possibly have heard it there were four grunts of approval from the verandah.

Raziah, the ball-boy, was slender; his flapping blue sports shirt and faded wax-print sarong made him look careless and almost comic. He was taller than Shimura and, as Shimura turned and walked to the net to meet him, the contrast was marked — the loose-limbed gait of the Malay in his rubber flip-flops, the compact movements of the Japanese who made his prowl forward into a swift bow of salutation.

Raziah said, "You can play me."

Shimura hesitated and before he replied he looked around in disappointment and resignation, as if he suspected he might be accused of something shameful. Then he said, "Okay, let's go."

"Now watch him run," said Evans, raising his glass of beer.

Raziah went to the baseline and dropped his sarong. He was wearing a pair of tennis shorts. He kicked off his flip-flops and put on white sneakers — new ones that looked large and dazzling in the sunlight. Raziah laughed out loud; he knew he had been transformed.

Squibb said, "Tony, you're a bloody genius."

Raziah won the toss and served. Raziah was seventeen; for seven of those years he had been a ball-boy, and he had learned the game by watching members play. Later, with a cast-off racket, he began playing in the early morning, before anyone was up. Evans had seen him in one of these six o'clock matches and, impressed by Raziah's speed and backhand, taught him to serve and showed him the fine points of the game. He inspired in him the psychic alertness and confidence that makes tennis champions. Evans, unmarried, had used his bachelor's idleness as a charitable pledge and gave this energy and optimism to Raziah, who became his pet and student and finally his partner. And Evans promised that he would, one of these years, put Raziah up for membership if he proved himself; he had so far withheld club membership from the Malay, although the boy had beaten him a number of times.

Raziah played a deceptively awkward game; the length of his arms made him appear to swing wildly; he was fast, but he often stumbled trying to stop. After the first set it was clear that everyone had underestimated Shimura. Raziah smashed serves at him, Shimura returned them forcefully, without apparent effort, and Shimura won the first two sets six-love. Changing ends, Raziah shrugged at the verandah as if to say, "I'm doing the best I can."

Evans said, "Raziah's a slow starter. He needs to win a few games to get his confidence up."

But he lost the first three games of the third set. Then Shimura, eager to finish him off, rushed the net and saw two of Raziah's drop shots land out of reach. When Raziah won that game, and the next — breaking Shimura's serve — there was a triumphant howl from the verandah. Raziah waved, and Shimura, who had been smiling, turned to see four men at the rail, the Chinese waiters on the steps, and crouching just under the verandah, two Tamil gardeners — everyone gazing with the intensity of jurors.

Shimura must have guessed that something was up. He reacted by playing angrily, slicing vicious shots at Raziah, or else lifting slow balls just over the net to drop hardly without a bounce at Raziah's feet. The pretense of the casual match was abandoned; the kitchen staff gathered along the sidelines and others — mostly Malay — stood at the hedge, cheering. There was laughter when Shimura slipped, applause when the towel fell from his neck.

What a good story a victory would have made! But nothing in Ayer Hitam was ever so neat. It would have been perfect revenge, a kind of romantic battle — the lanky local boy with his old racket, making a stand against the intruder; the drama of vindicating not only his own reputation as a potentially great tennis player, but indeed the dignity of the entire club. The match had its charms: Raziah had a way of chewing and swallowing and working his Adam's apple at Shimura when the Japanese lost a point; Raziah talked as he played, a muttering narration that was meant to unnerve his opponent; and he took his time serving, shrugging his shoulders and bouncing the ball. But it was a very short contest, for as Evans and the others watched with hopeful and judging solemnity, Raziah lost.

The astonishing thing was that none of the club staff, and

none of Raziah's friends, seemed to realize that he had lost. They were still laughing and cheering and congratulating themselves long after Shimura had aced his last serve past Raziah's knees; and not for the longest time did the festive mood change.

Evans jumped to the court. Shimura was clamping his press to his racket, mopping his face. Seeing Evans he started to walk away.

"I'd like a word with you," said Evans.

Shimura looked downcast; sweat and effort had plastered his hair close to his head, and his fatigue was curiously like sadness, as if he had been beaten. He had missed the hatred before, hadn't noticed us; but the laughter, the sudden crowd, the charade of the challenge match had showed him how much he was hated and how much trouble we had gone to in order to prove it. He said, "So."

Evans was purple. "You come to the Club quite a bit, I see."

"Yes."

"I think you ought to be acquainted with the rules."

"I have not broken any rules."

Evans said curtly, "You didn't sign in your guest."

Shimura bowed and walked to the clubhouse. Evans glared at Raziah; Raziah shook his head, then went for his sarong, and putting it on he became again a Malay of the town, one of numerous idlers who'd never be members of the Ayer Hitam Club.

The following day Shimura left. We never saw him again. For a month Evans claimed it as a personal victory. But that was short-lived, for the next news was of Raziah's defection. Shimura had invited him to Kuala Lumpur and entered him in the Federation Championship, and the jersey Raziah wore when he won a respectable third prize had the name of Shimura's company on it, an electronics firm. And there was to be more. Shimura put him up for membership in the Selangor Club, and so we knew that it was only a matter of time before Raziah returned to Ayer Hitam to claim reciprocal privileges as a guest member. And even those who hated Shimura and criticized his lob were forced to admire the cleverness of his Oriental revenge.

12. Reggie Woo

His FATHER, Woo Boh Swee, had chased after the English in that shy, breathless Chinese way, hating the necessity of it and making his embarrassment into haste. He had gone from Canton to Hong Kong to work on an English ship and later had come to Ayer Hitam to supply the rubber estates with provisions. But the rubber price had fallen, many English and American families left the town, and the Chinese who replaced them imported or grew their own food; so he started City Bar.

It was the biggest coffee shop in town, the meeting place for a secret society — but the gang was only dangerous to other Chinese and did not affect Woo's regular trade, the remaining English planters, and the Tamil rubber tappers. Woo — or "City Bar" as he was known — was thoroughly Chinese; he was a chain smoker, he played mahjong on a back table of the shop, he observed all the Chinese festivals with *ang pows*. The shop smelled of dusty bottles and bean curd, and dark greasy ducks and glazed pork strips hung on hooks in the front window. He and his wife were great gamblers, and they had two children.

The children went to different schools. It was as if, this once, the Woos were hedging, making an each-way bet. The girl, Jin Bee, was at the Chinese primary school; the boy,

Reggie, had been to the Anglo-Chinese school, then to Raffles Institution and the University of Singapore. He was the English child; he played cricket and tennis and was a member of the Ayer Hitam Club. He had distinguished himself by appearing in the Footlighters' production of Maugham's play, *The Letter*. It was the first play to attract a local audience; it ran for a week, and Reggie's picture was in the *Johore Mail*. That picture, bright yellow with age, was taped to the wall of City Bar. Everyone had hopes for Reggie. He was that odd figure you sometimes see in the East, the person who leaves his race behind, who goes to school and returns home English. Ayer Hitam was not an easy place to be English, but Reggie, an actor, had certain advantages. He was right for the part. And though drinks at the Club were more expensive than at City Bar, Reggie was at the Club, drinking, nearly every evening.

One night I saw him alone in the lounge. He looked like an actor who hadn't been warned that his play was canceled; dressed up, solitary, he was a figure of neglect, and his expectant look was changing into one of desolation. I joined him, we talked about the heat, and after a while I told him he ought to get a scholarship to study overseas.

"I wouldn't mind!" He brushed his hair out of his eyes. "How do I go about it?"

"That depends," I said. "What's your field?"

"Philosophy."

I was prepared to be surprised, but I was unprepared for that. It was his clothes, narrow trousers, pointed shoes, a pink shirt, and a silk scarf knotted at his throat. "It would be strange," I said. "A Chinese from Malaysia going to the States to study Oriental philosophy."

"Why do you say Oriental philosophy?" He looked offended in a rather formal way.

"Just a wild guess."

"A bad guess," he said. "Whitehead, Russell, Kant." He showed me three well-manicured fingers. Then a fourth. "Karl Popper."

"You're interested in them, are you?"

"I studied them," he said. "I wrote on the mind-body problem."

"I'll see what I can do."

The Fulbright forms had to come from Kuala Lumpur, so it was a week before I looked for him again, and when I looked he wasn't there — not at the Club and not at City Bar. "In Singapore," his father said. "Got business."

There were eight or ten people at the Club the night Reggie came back. I noticed they were all Footlighters. I waited until they left him — they had been gathered around him, talking loudly — and then I told him I had the forms.

"Something's come up," he said. He grinned. "I'm going to be in a film. That's why I was in Singapore. Auditioning. And I got the part-*lah*."

"Congratulations," I said. "What film is it?"

"*Man's Fate*," he said. "I'm playing Ch'en. I've always adored Malraux and I love acting. Now I can draw on my philosophy background as well. So you see, it's perfect."

"What does your father think about it?"

"It's a job — he's keen," said Reggie. "It's my big chance, and it could lead to bigger parts."

"Hollywood," I said.

He smiled. "I would never go to Hollywood. False life, no sense of values. I plan to make London my base, but if the money was good I might go to the States for a few weeks at a time."

"When are they going to make *Man's Fate*?"

"Shooting starts in Singapore in a month's time."

And the way he said *shooting* convinced me that the Ful-bright forms would never be used.

After that I heard a lot about Reggie at the Club. Lady-smith, the English teacher, said, "City Bar's son's done all right for himself," and Reggie was always in sight, in new clothes, declining drinks. Squibb said, "These things never come off," and some people referred to Reggie as "that fruit." But most were pleased. The Footlighters said, "I can say I knew you when," and cautioned him about the small print in contracts, and when they filed in at dusk for the first drink they greeted him with, "How's our film star?"

Reggie's reply was, "I had a letter just the other day." He said this week after week, giving the impression of a constant flow of mail, keeping him up to date. But I realized, as his manner became more abrupt and diffident, that it was always the same letter.

Then a job came up at the Anglo-Chinese school: a history teacher was needed. Reggie's name was mentioned, it was his old school, he was out of work. But he turned it down. "I can't commit myself to a teaching post with this film in the pipeline!" He lost his temper with the Chinese barman who mistook tonic for soda. He shouted at the ball-boys on the tennis courts. Like a film star, people said.

Twice a week, when the program changed at the Capitol Cinema in Johore Bahru, Reggie made the sixty-mile drive in his father's van, usually with an English girl from the Club. There were rumors of romance, even talk of marriage; names were mentioned, Millsap's daughter, Squibb's niece. Reggie spoke of going to London.

One day he was gone. I noticed his absence because the Club was holding rehearsals for a new play, and Reggie, who had not missed a major production since *The Letter*, was not in the cast. It was said he was in Singapore, and I assumed they were shooting *Man's Fate*.

Sometime later, the glimpse of a face being averted in a post office crowd reminded me of Reggie. I mentioned him to my *peon*, Peeraswami.

"At City Bar," said Peeraswami.

"Then he *is* back."

I remember the night I went over to offer my congratulations, and I could find it on a calendar even now, because there was a full moon over a cloud that hung like a dragon in the sky. The usual nighttime crowd of drinkers and idlers were at City Bar. I looked for the figure in the scarf and sunglasses I had seen so many times in the Club, but all I saw were Chinese gesturing with coffee cups and Tamils drinking toddy — everyone in short-sleeved white shirts. A hot night in a Malaysian town has a particular bittersweet taste; the chatter and noise in that place seemed to make the taste stronger. I fought my way into the bar and saw Woo Boh Swee, scowling at the cash register.

"Where's Reggie?"

He jerked his thumb inside but stared at me in an excluding way. When I saw Reggie in the back, hunched over the mahjong table in the short-sleeved shirt that made him anonymous, his legs folded, kicking a rubber scandal up and down, I knew it would be an intrusion to go any further. I heard him abuse his opponent in sharp, unmistakably Cantonese jeers as he banged down a mahjong tile. I left before he caught sight of me and went back to the Club, crossing the road with that sinking feeling you get at a national boundary or an unguarded frontier.

13. Conspirators

NOT ONE PERSON I had known in Africa was my age — they were either much older or much younger. That could hardly have been true, and yet that was how it appeared to me. I was very young.

The Indian seemed old; I had never spoken to him; I did not know his name. He was one of those people, common in small towns, whom one sees constantly, and who, like a feature of the landscape, become anonymous because they are never out of view, like a newspaper seller or a particular cripple. He was dark, always alone, and threadbare in an indestructible way. He used to show up at the door of the Gujarati restaurant where I ate, The Hindu Lodge, an old man with a cardboard box of Indian sweets, and he said — it was his one word of English — "Sweetmeats."

In my two-year tour in Uganda I saw him hundreds of times, in that open doorway, blinking because of the flies near his face. No one bought the food he had in the dirty cardboard box. He showed the box, said his word, and then went away. It was as if he was doing it against his will: he had been sent by someone conspiring to find out what we would do with him, a test of our sympathy. We did nothing. If anyone had asked me about him at the time I think I would have said that I found him terribly reassuring. But no one asked; no one saw him.

Ayer Hitam, half a world away, had her Indian conspirators, but being political, they had names. Rao had been arrested on a political charge. It was said that he was a communist. I found the description slightly absurd in that small town, like the cheese-colored building they called the Ministry of Works or the bellyache everyone referred to as dysentery. In Malaysia a communist meant someone either very poor or very safe, who gathered with others in a kind of priestly cabal, meeting at night over a table littered with boring papers and high-minded pamphlets to reheat their anger. I could imagine the futile talk, the despair of the ritual which had its more vulgar counterpart in the lounge of the Ayer Hitam Club. It was said that the communists wanted to poison the Sultan's polo-ponies and nationalize the palmoil estates. They were people seeking to be arrested. Arrest was their victory, and in that sense they were like early Christians, needing to be persecuted because they wished to prove their courage. They were conspirators; they inspired others in conspiracy against them. Most Malays were superstitious about them. To speak too much of the communists was to give their faith an importance it didn't deserve. But when they were caught they were imprisoned.

Rao had been in prison for some time. The Embassy told me of his release and how he had returned to Ayer Hitam. I was ashamed to admit that I had never heard of him. My people gave me a few facts: Rao had been a real firebrand; he had given public speeches; he had started a cell in the mission school; he was a confidant of the Chinese goldsmiths who were, somehow, Maoists; he had caused at least two riots in town. I was skeptical but interested: large affairs, wild talk — but the town looked small and tame and too sparsely populated to support a riot. An unlawful assembly, perhaps, but not a riot.

Virtually everyone I knew suspected me of being a spy. I was seen as a legitimate conspirator. In a small way I suppose I was. My information was negligible: I was sorry it mattered so little. It would have been encouraging to know that my cables were eagerly awaited and quickly acted upon. But what I sent was filed and never queried, never crucial. I was in the wrong place. I could have reported on the Chinese goldsmiths, but I knew better. Theirs was a sentimental attachment to China, their nationalism the nostalgia of souvenirs, like calendar pictures of Tien-An-Men Square in Peking. I reminded myself that an Italian in the United States would have a feeling for Italy no matter who governed. It was the same with the Chinese. My cables were as eventless as the town. I knew I didn't count.

I was surprised when the Political Section asked me to see Rao privately and find out what he was up to. I assumed that if I approved him he might be offered a scholarship to study in the States. There was no better catch than an ex-communist. People would listen to him, and he could always have the last word. He knew the other side: he had been there. If I flunked him, I knew — it was the system — he would be unemployable.

Rao worked, I found out, in the office of the town's solicitor, Francis Ratnasingham. I spoke to Francis and he said that he had no objection to my talking to Rao during office hours: "He will be flattered by your interest."

Rao came into the room carrying a tray of papers. It looked for a moment like a shallow box of food. He held it out and gave me a wan smile.

"They said you wanted to talk to me."

His voice was flat and had a hint of defeat in it, which

contradicted what I had heard about him, the speeches, the riots he'd caused. He was heavy — jail weight, like the useless bulk of a farm turkey. He looked underexercised and slow.

"I said, "I don't want to take you away from your work."

"It doesn't make any difference."

I tried not to stare at his big soft face. This was a firebrand! He looked at the tray, as if surprised to see it in his hands, then placed it on a desk.

"I hope you're not busy."

He said, "Francis told me to expect you."

Ratnasingham's office was in Victoria Chambers on the main street, Jalan Besar. I said we could have a drink at the Club. Rao suggested tea at City Bar, and it was there that he said, "I reckon you saw me on television in K.L."

"No," I said. "When was that?"

"Two months ago."

"What did you do?"

"I recanted." He smiled.

I stared: *recanted?*

He said, "I had to do it twice. They didn't like my first try — they said I didn't sound sincere enough."

I had heard that political prisoners had been made to recant, but I didn't realize the government televised it. Rao said it was one of the conditions of release.

"How long were you in jail?"

"Seven years."

I couldn't hide my astonishment. And I put it in personal terms — seven years was the length of my whole Foreign Service career. So Rao and I were the same age, conspiring differently.

He said, "You don't believe me."

"It's a hell of a long time to be in jail."

"Yes." He stirred his tea. "But I took lessons. I did correspondence courses. I studied. It helped the time pass." He shrugged. "How do you like Malaysia?"

"I'm enjoying myself." This sounded frivolous. "Maybe I shouldn't be."

"Why not? It's a nice country. We have our problems. But — " He shrugged again, and laughed. This time his amusement seemed real.

"What were you studying in prison?"

"Law — an external degree from London University. They sent me books and lessons. They were very good about it. They didn't charge me anything."

"You got the degree?"

"Oh, no," he said, and he sighed. "There were too many interruptions. I couldn't keep the written material in my cell without permission. I had to request it from the warders and they needed a chit from the prison governor. One day they would give me a book but no paper. The next they'd give me paper but no pencil or book. I'd ask for a pencil. They'd give it, but take away the paper."

"That's torture," I said.

"Maybe," he said. "It was a problem."

"But they were doing it deliberately!"

He nodded. I searched for anger on his face. There was only that dull look of amusement. He said, "It made the time pass."

"I can see why you didn't get the degree in prison. What a relief it must be to have your own paper and pens and books and make your own rules for a change."

"I don't make any rules," he said, and sounded defensive.

"I mean, about studying," I said quickly.

"I don't study."

"But you said you were working for a degree."

"In prison," he said. "It was important at the time, even that business about paper but no pencil. When I was released, I stopped. I didn't need it."

I said, "You could continue your studies in the States."

He shook his head.

"Don't you want to leave the country?"

"It's them. They wouldn't give me a passport."

"You could get a traveling document. I might be able to help you with that."

He smiled, as if he had been told all of this before.

"Why don't you leave?"

He said, "Because they wouldn't let me back into the country."

"So you can never leave?"

"I don't say never. I don't think about time anymore."

"Do you mind me asking you these questions?"

He said softly, "I know who you are."

"I would genuinely like to help you."

He laughed again, the authentic laugh, not the mechanical one. "Maybe you could have helped me, seven years ago. Now, no."

"What are the other conditions of your release? You had to recant, you're forbidden to leave the country — "

"You don't understand," he said. "I recanted voluntarily. I don't want to leave the country. It's my choice."

"But the alternative was staying in jail."

"Let's say it took me seven years to make up my mind." He stared at me and frowned. "It wasn't a hasty decision."

He was impenetrable. And he looked it, too. He was not tall, but he was large, square-headed, and had a thickness of flesh that wasn't muscle. I could not help thinking that he had deliberately become like this as a reproach to all action; it was his way of sulking.

He said, "I know some chaps who were in even longer than me, so I don't complain."

This was news. "You keep in touch with other prisoners?"

"Oh, yes," he said lightly. "We're members of the Ex-Detainees Association."

"You have a club?"

He nodded. "I'm the secretary."

I might have known. Ayer Hitam was full of clubs — Chinese clan associations, secret societies, communist cells, Indian sports clubs, the South Malaysia Pineapple Growers' Association, the Muslim League, the Legion of Mary, the Methodist Ramblers; and I was in one myself. No one lived in the town, really; people just went to club meetings there.

Rao looked at his watch. He said, "Five o'clock."

"I've kept you."

"It doesn't matter. I don't have any work to do. I'm just a file clerk. They won't sack me."

"Have another cup of tea. Or what about splitting a large Anchor?"

"I don't drink beer," he said. "I learned to do without it."

I couldn't ask him the other thing, how he had gone so long without a woman. But I was curious, and when he said "I should be heading home," I offered him a ride.

In the car he spoke to Abubaker gently in Malay, and Abubaker laughed. For a moment they looked like conspirators sharing a secret. But Rao, as if guessing at my interest, said, "I told him I wanted to buy his posh car."

"Do you?"

"Not at all."

We drove for several miles in silence.

Rao said, "It was a joke, you see."

His house, a small two-room bungalow, unfenced, exposed

to the sun, was directly on the road — an odd place to be in so empty a landscape.

Rao said, "Will you come in?"

He was being polite. He didn't want me.

I said, "All right. But just for a minute."

After the business of making tea and his carefully setting out a dish of savories that were like macaroni coated with hot pepper, there seemed nothing to say. The room was bare. It did not even have the calendar most of the houses in Ayer Hitam displayed. It had no mirror, no pictures. It was, surprisingly, like a jail cell. He lived alone; there was no sign of a woman, no servants' quarters, no books.

A timber truck went by and shook the windows.

"I like it here," said Rao, almost defiantly.

He left the room and came back with a large plastic-covered book with thick pages, a photograph album. He showed me an old blurred snapshot of a dark schoolboy in white shorts. He said, "That's me." He showed me a picture of a Chinese man. "He was one of the warders." A palm tree. "That's Mersing. There are beautiful islands there. You should visit." A battered car. "That belonged to my uncle. He died." There were no more pictures. Rao said, "When I have some free time I take out this album and look at the pictures."

But they were pictures of nothing. He had no fire. I had suspected him of keeping something from me; but he hadn't, he was concealing nothing, he had been destroyed.

He said, "I told you I couldn't help you."

And I left. I was driving back when I remembered that poor Indian in Kampala. I hadn't thought of him for years. I was sad, sadder than I had been for a long time, because I knew now he was dead.

It took me weeks to write my report on Rao. I had to

suppress the implications of what I'd seen. I put down the obvious facts, and — saying that he'd returned to normal life — invented a happy man, whom prison had cured of all passion. The conspiracy was complete. But I was glad he had showed no interest in a scholarship or a travel grant, because when I reflected on Rao I saw his transformation as the ultimate deceit. I knew I would not have trusted him an inch.

14. The Johore Murders

THE FIRST VICTIM was a British planter, and everyone at the Club said what a shame it was that after fifteen years in the country he was killed just four days before he planned to leave. He had no family, he lived alone; until he was murdered no one knew very much about him. Murder is the grimmest, briefest fame. If the second victim, a month later, had not been an American I probably would not have given the Johore murders a second thought, and I certainly would not have been involved in the business. But who would have guessed that Ismail Garcia was an American?

The least dignified thing that can happen to a man is to be murdered. If he dies in his sleep he gets a respectful obituary and perhaps a smiling portrait; it is how we all want to be remembered. But murder is the great exposer: here is the victim in his torn underwear, face down on the floor, unpaid bills on his dresser, a meager shopping list, some loose change, and worst of all the fact that he is alone. Investigation reveals what he did that day — it all matters — his habits are examined, his behavior scrutinized, his trunks rifled, and a balance sheet is drawn up at the hospital giving the contents of his stomach. Dying, the last private act we perform, is made public: the murder victim has no secrets.

So, somewhere in Garcia's house, a passport was found, an

American one, and that was when the Malaysian police contacted the Embassy in Kuala Lumpur. I was asked to go down for the death certificate, personal effects, and anything that might be necessary for the report to his next of kin. I intended it to be a stopover, a day in Johore, a night in Singapore, and then back to Ayer Hitam. Peeraswami had a brother in Johore; Abubaker, my driver, said he wanted to pray at the Johore mosque; we pushed off early one morning, Abubaker at the wheel, Peeraswami playing with the car radio. I was in the back seat going over newspaper clippings of the two murders.

In most ways they were the same. Each victim was a foreigner, unmarried, lived alone in a house outside town, and had been a resident for some years. In neither case was there any sign of a forced entry or a robbery. Both men were poor, both men had been mutilated. They looked to me like acts of Chinese revenge. But on planters? In Malaysia it was the Chinese *towkay* who was robbed, kidnaped, or murdered, not the expatriate planters who lived from month to month on provisioners' credit and chit-signing in bars. There were two differences: Tibbets was British and Ismail Garcia was American. And one other known fact: Tibbets, at the time of his death, was planning to go back to England.

A two-hour drive through rubber estates took us into Johore, and then we were speeding along the shore of the Straits, past the lovely casuarina trees and the high houses on the leafy bluff that overlooks the swampland and the marshes on the north coast of Singapore. I dropped Peeraswami at his brother's house, which was in one of the wilder suburbs of Johore and with a high chain-link fence around it to assure even greater seclusion. Abubaker scrambled out at the mosque after giving me directions to the police headquarters.

Garcia's effects were in a paper bag from a Chinese shop. I signed for them and took them to a table to examine: a cheap watch, a cheap ring, a copy of the Koran, a birth certificate, the passport.

"We left the clothes behind," said Detective-Sergeant Yusof. "We just took the valuables."

Valuables: there wasn't five dollars' worth of stuff in the bag.

"Was there any money?"

"He had no money. We're not treating it as robbery."

"What *are* you treating it as?"

"Homicide, probably by a friend."

"Some friend."

"He knew the murderer, so did Tibbets. You will believe me when you see the houses."

I almost did. Garcia's house was completely surrounded by a high fence, and Yusof said that Tibbets's fence was even higher. It was not unusual; every large house in Malaysian cities had an unclimbable fence or a wall with spikes of glass cemented on to the top.

"The lock wasn't broken, the house wasn't tampered with," said Yusof. "So we are calling it a sex crime."

"I thought you were calling it a homicide."

Yusof smirked at me. "We have a theory. The Englishmen who live here get funny ideas. Especially the ones who live alone. Some of them take Malay mistresses, the other ones go around with Chinese boys."

"Not Malay boys?"

Yusof said, "We do not do such things."

"You say Englishmen do, but Garcia was an American."

"He was single," said Yusof.

"I'm single," I said.

"We couldn't find any sign of a mistress."

"I thought you were looking for a murderer."

"That's what I'm trying to say," said Yusof. "These queers are very secretive. They get jealous. They fight with their boyfriends. The body was mutilated — that tells me a Chinese boy is involved."

"So you don't think it had anything to do with money?"

"Do you know what the rubber price is?"

"As a matter of fact, I do."

"And that's not all," said Yusof. "This man Garcia — do you know what he owed his provisioner? Eight hundred-over dollars! Tibbets was owing five hundred."

I said, "Maybe the provisioner did it."

"Interesting," said Yusof. "We can work on that."

Tibbets was English, so over lunch I concentrated on Garcia. There was a little dossier on him from the Alien Registration Office. Born 1922 in the Philippines; fought in World War II; took out American citizenship in Guam, came to Malaysia in 1954, converted to Islam and changed his name. From place to place, complicating his identity, picking up a nationality here, a name there, a religion somewhere else. And why would he convert? A woman, of course. No man changed his religion to live with another man. I didn't believe he was a homosexual, and though there was no evidence to support it I didn't rule out the possibility of robbery. In all this there were two items that interested me — the birth certificate and the passport. The birth certificate was brown with age, the passport new and unused.

Why would a man who had changed his religion and lived in a country for nearly twenty years have a new passport?

After lunch I rang police headquarters and asked for Yusof.

"We've got the provisioner," he said. "I think you might be right. He was also Tibbets's provisioner — both men owed him money. He is helping us with our inquiries."

"What a pompous phrase for torture," I said, but before Yusof could reply I added, "About Garcia — I figure he was planning to leave the country."

Yusof cackled into the phone. "Not at all! We talked to his employer — Garcia had a permanent and pensionable contract."

"Then why did he apply for a passport two weeks ago?"

"It is the law. He must be in possession of a valid passport if he is an expatriate."

I said, "I'd like to talk to his employer."

Yusof gave me the name of the man, Tan See Leng, owner of the Tai-Hwa Rubber Estate. I went over that afternoon. At first Tan refused to see me, but when I sent him my card with the consulate address and the American eagle on it, he rushed out of his office and apologized. He was a thin evasive man with spiky hair, and though he pretended not to be surprised when I said Garcia was an American national I could tell this was news to him. He said he knew nothing about Garcia, apart from the fact that he'd been a good foreman. He'd never see him socially. He confirmed that Garcia lived behind an impenetrable fence.

"Who owned the house?"

"He did."

"That's something," I said. "I suppose you knew he was leaving the country."

"He was not leaving. He was wucking."

"It would help if you told me the truth," I said.

Tan's bony face tightened with anger. He said, "Perhaps he intended to leave. I do not know."

"I take it business isn't so good."

"The rubber price is low, some planters are switching to oil palm. But the price will rise if we are patient."

"What did you pay Garcia?"

"Two thousand a month. He was on permanent terms — he signed one of the old contracts. We were very generous in those days with expatriates."

"But he could have broken the contract."

"Some men break."

"Up in Ayer Hitam they have something called a 'golden handshake.' If they want to get rid of a foreigner they offer him a chunk of money as compensation for loss of career."

"That is Ayer Hitam," said Tan. "This is Johore."

"And they always pay cash, because it's against the law to take that much money out of the country. No banks. Just a suitcase full of Straits dollars."

Tan said nothing.

I said, "I don't think Garcia or Tibbets were queer. I think this was robbery, pure and simple."

"The houses were not broken into."

"So the papers say," I said. "It's the only thing I don't understand. Both men were killed at home during the day."

"Mister," said Tan. "You should leave this to the police."

"You swear you didn't give Garcia a golden handshake?"

"That is against the law, as you say."

"It's not as serious as murder, is it?"

In the course of the conversation, Tan had turned to wood. I was sure he was lying, but he stuck to his story. I decided to have nothing more to do with the police or Yusof and instead to go back to the house of Peeraswami's brother, to test a theory of my own.

The house bore many similarities to Garcia's and to what I knew of Tibbets's. It was secluded, out of town, rather characterless, and the high fence was topped with barbed wire. Sathya, Peeraswami's brother, asked me how I liked Johore. I told him that I liked it so much I wanted to spend a few days there, but that I didn't want the Embassy to know where I was. I asked him if he would put me up.

"Oh, yes," he said. "You are welcome. But you would be more comfortable in a hotel."

"It's much quieter here."

"It is the country life. We have no car."

"It's just what I'm looking for."

After I was shown to my bedroom I excused myself and went to the offices of the *Johore Mail*, read the classified ads for the previous few weeks and placed an ad myself. For the next two days I explored Johore, looked over the Botanical Gardens and the Sultan's mosque, and ingratiated myself with Sathya and his family. I had arrived on a Friday. On Monday I said to Sathya, "I'm expecting a phone call today."

Sathya said, "This is your house."

"I feel I ought to do something in return," I said. "I have a driver and a car — I don't need them today. Why don't you use them? Take your wife and children over to Singapore and enjoy yourself."

He hesitated, but finally I persuaded him. Abubaker, on the other hand, showed an obvious distaste for taking an Indian family out for the day.

"Peeraswami," I said. "I'd like you to stay here with me."

"*Tuan*," he said, agreeing. Sathya and the others left. I locked the gate behind them and sat by the telephone to wait.

There were four phone calls. Three of the callers I discouraged by describing the location, the size of the house, the tiny garden, the work I said had to be done on the roof. And I gave the same story to the last caller, but he was insistent and eager to see it. He said he'd be right over.

Rawlins was the name he gave me. He came in a new car, gave me a hearty greeting, and was not at all put off by the slightly ramshackle appearance of the house. He smoked a cheroot which had stained his teeth and the center swatch of his mustache a sticky yellow, and he walked around with one hand cupped, tapping ashes into his palm.

"You're smart not to use an agent," he said, looking over the house. "These estate agents are bloody thieves."

I showed him the garden, the lounge, the kitchen.

He sniffed and said, "You like curry."

"My cook's an Indian." He went silent, glanced around suspiciously, and I added, "I gave him the day off."

"You lived here long?"

"Ten years. I'm chucking it. I've been worried about selling this place ever since I broke my contract."

"Rubber?" he said, and spat a fragment of the cheroot into his hand.

"Yes," I said. "I was manager of an estate up in Kluang."

He asked me the price and when I told him he said, "I can manage that." He took out a checkbook. "I'll give you a deposit now and the balance when contracts are exchanged. We'll put our lawyers in touch and Bob's your uncle. Got a pen?"

I went to the desk and opened a drawer, but as I rummaged he said, "Okay, turn around slow and put your hands up."

I did as I was told and heard the cheroot hitting the floor. Above the kris Rawlins held his face was fierce and twisted. In such an act a man reverts; his face was pure monkey, threatening teeth and eyes. He said, "Now hand it over."

"What is this?" I said. "What do you want?"

"Your money, all of it, your handshake."

"I don't have any money."

"They always lie," he said. "They always fight, and then I have to do them. Just make it easy this time. The money — "

But he said no more, for Peeraswami in his bare feet crept behind him from the broom cupboard where he had been hiding and brought a cast-iron frying pan down so hard on his skull that I thought for a moment I saw a crack show in the man's forehead. We tied Rawlins up with Sathya's neckties and then I rang Yusof.

On the way to police headquarters, where Yusof insisted the corpse be delivered, I said, "This probably would not have happened if you didn't have such strict exchange control regulations."

"So it was robbery," said Yusof, "but how did he know Tibbets and Garcia had had golden handshakes?"

"He guessed. There was no risk involved. He knew they were leaving the country because they'd put their houses up for sale. Expatriates who own houses here have been in the country a long time, which means they're taking a lot of money out in a suitcase. You should read the paper."

"I read the paper," said Yusof. "Malay and English press."

"I mean the classified ads, where it says, 'Expatriate-owned house for immediate sale. Leaving the country. No agents.' Tibbets and Garcia placed that ad, and so did I."

Yusof said, "I should have done that. I could have broken this case."

"I doubt it — he wouldn't have done business with a Malay," I said. "But remember, if a person says he wants to buy your house you let him in. It's the easiest way for a burglar to enter — through the front door. If he's a white man in this country no one suspects him. We're supposed to trust each other. As soon as I realized it had something to do with the sale of a house I knew the murderer would be white."

"He didn't know they were alone."

"The wife and kids always fly out first, especially if daddy's breaking currency regulations."

"You foreigners know all the tricks."

"True," I said. "If he was a Malay or a Chinese I probably wouldn't have been able to catch him." I tapped my head. "I understand the mind of the West."

15. The Tiger's Suit

ALMOST the worst corpse I've ever seen was that of a Malay woman, an epileptic, who, out planting rice in a field, had had a fit and tumbled into a flooded ditch. She was alone, and as soon as she was submerged the horseleeches swarmed beneath her loose blouse and over her legs and face. She hadn't drowned; she died from loss of blood, it had been sucked by those fattened leeches. They still clung to her, black with her blood, after she was hauled out. Her color was the most awful gray, like a dead sea creature with salt in her veins. Then the leeches were struck by the air and they peeled off and sank in the ditch, leaving the woman covered with welts the shape of watchstraps. It gave Ayer Hitam a week of fame. People came from all over to look at the ditch, and even now you can see the spot clearly because no one would plant rice near it after the tragedy. It had the makings of a horror story: the corpse found with its blood sucked, an investigation, some detective work, the news that she was an epileptic, and the chilling truth — leeches.

I never thought I would see anything worse; then the corpse of the child turned up, Aziza binte Salim. I suppose what made it particularly dreadful was her age — not more than seven — and the fact that she was a girl. Most people are apprehensive about their daughters; Malays turn this apprehension into paranoia, or at least underpin it with the ferocity of Islamic suspicion. Aziza was a prize, a cute round-faced girl with jet-black hair. She lived in the *kampong* at the northern end of the town, which bordered on the derelict rubber estate. The Malays there had repossessed the huts of the Tamil rubber tappers, shading them with banana groves. I often used to walk out that way in the late afternoon when the Consulate closed, to limber up for tennis. My walks were a displacement activity: I would have had a drink if I had gone to the Club after work; then another drink, and another, and no tennis. Though I never knew her name, I went through the *kampong* afterward and — how shall I put it? — I noticed she was missing. Then I remembered her laughing face.

The monsoon was late that year, so late it looked as if the rice shoots would never be planted. The fields had been prepared in that clumsy traditional way, by buffaloes dragging the metal ploughs through the water, stirring the mud. But weeks later there was still no rain, and the paddy fields were beginning to show the ridges of the empty furrows as the water level dropped. The ditches dried and the embankments came apart as the grass that knitted them together died. A sad sight: the quilt of drying fields that had been so green in the previous planting, the sun's slow fire bringing death.

While the agricultural officers were deliberating over their clipboards (one American-trained Malay used to come to the Club and say, "These guys haven't got a chance" —I wanted to sock him in the jaw), the *kampong* was deciding things its own way.

I had the story from Peeraswami. As soon as it became clear that the situation was desperate, the Malay rice farmers met and decided to bring their problem to a *bomoh* — a medicine man — whose hut was deep in the bush, not far from the village of aboriginal Laruts who acted as his messengers. It was a part of the jungle where not even the Sultan's tax collectors showed their faces. This *bomoh*, Noor, had a reputation. Later when I saw him in court he looked a most mild man, somewhat comic in his old-fashioned wire spectacles.

But he scared the life out of Peeraswami, who said that the Malays from the *kampong* had sworn that no one should reveal their identities — they took a vow of secrecy before they set out. Most of the stories about the *bomoh* Noor came from the Laruts, who spoke of goats that had disappeared and odd howlings from the *bomoh's* hut. The Laruts had never engaged him, but the reason was simple: Noor was expensive. He asked the visiting Malays to make a contribution before he allowed them in.

The next thing he said was that the *kampong* was cursed: the curse was keeping the monsoon away.

They expected to hear that. They would have been surprised if he had said anything else. But how to cure it?

"There is always a cure," said the *bomoh* Noor. "Can you afford it?"

They said yes, of course, but when the *bomoh* only smiled and said nothing else for several minutes they began wondering if their answer should have been no.

"Three hundred dollars," said Noor, finally.

At that time, the exchange rate was three to one, Straits dollars to American green. But this was quite a sum to simple rice farmers who, long before the next harvest, would be living on credit from the Chinese shops. They had a fear, common in agricultural societies, of being uprooted and driven to a hostile part of the country to begin again. They asked the *bomoh* his terms.

"Half the money now, the balance when it is finished."

"When the rain falls," said one man.

"When it is finished there will be rain."

The strange distancing construction of the Malay verbs made them inquire further: "You're going to do it yourself?"

"It will be done," said the *bomoh*, using the same courtly remoteness.

"By you?"

"It is tiger's work," said the old man. He smiled and showed his black teeth. Even the most menacing *bomoh* had an access of comedy — it could be as effective a curative as fear. The ramshackle hut, the clay bowls of beaks and feathers, the stink of decayed roots had, mingled with the riddle of their threat, an element of the clownish. But according to Peeraswami no one laughed. The old man said, "The money."

They handed over the hundred and fifty. The bills were counted and put in a strong-box. The old man gestured for them to sit down.

The sun continued hot, wilting the foliage of the elastic figs; the frangipanis lost their leaves, and the bougainvilleas at the Club took on a frail drooping look, rusted blossoms and slack leaves hanging from brittle branches. The dust was everywhere. The grass courts behind the Club were impossible, and I recall how an especially hard backhand shot would send the ball bouncing into my opponent's face with a great puff of red dust. This was bad, and most people said it would get worse. It was a suffocating business to take the shortest walk. I worked late just to be away from the Club and the temptation to drink heavily. The other members wilted visibly at tables, cursing the heat over glasses of beer. Ayer Hitam was parched, changed in color from the yellow stucco to the deep red of the risen dust, and the tires of the trishaws left marks in the sun-softened tar.

After another week I was drinking — my habitual anesthetic of gin. One lunchtime, on the club verandah, I heard a commotion — whoops, shouts, a great gabbling. Odd sounds in such exhausting weather. On the road beyond the Club's cricket ground were running people, twenty or more. They were gibbering and crying out, beating their way from a banana grove. The cries reached us, "*Matjan! Matjan!*"

At the next table Squibb said, "Something's up."

We went to the rail. The elderly Chinese Head Boy, Stanley Chee, crossed the verandah with a tray and towel. He peered at the road and cocked his head.

"It's a tiger," he said.

"Balls," said Squibb. "There hasn't been a tiger here for twenty years. Sure, you get them in Tapah, the Cameron Highlands, those places. They can feed there. But you never get them as far south as this. There's nothing for them to eat, and they've all been poached away."

"*Matjan!*" The word was clear.

"If it is a tiger," said Angela Miller, "I'd love to see it. But an Ayer Hitam tiger would probably look like the one in that Saki story — toothless and frightened."

Stanley Chee was still studying the mob in the road. He said, "This tiger killed someone."

"No," said Angela, touching her throat.

"They have the body — there, you can see them carrying it."

If it had been a car accident none of us would have gone near. Malays have been known to overturn a vehicle and kill the driver at the scene of an accident. But with Stanley's assurance that it was a tiger we left the verandah and met the procession.

And that is when I saw the corpse, which as I say was much worse than that poor epileptic's. It was clearly a small girl. She had been torn open, partially eaten — or at least frantically chewed — and flayed like a rabbit. Her blood stained the sheets they were carrying her in: red blossoms soaked it. Nor was that all, for just behind the first group there was another group, with a smaller sheet, and this bundle contained Aziza's head.

People were running from all directions, the Chinese from the shops, Peeraswami and his Tamil pals from the post office; and the Malays continued to shout while the impassive Stanley said, "They found her in the *lallang* like that — they think it was a tiger. She is the daughter of Salim the carpenter."

While we were standing there I got a sudden chill that made me hunch my shoulders. I thought it was simple fear and did not notice the sky darkening until it had gone almost black. Bizarre: but the monsoon is like that, bringing a dark twilight at noon. The bamboos started cracking against each other, the banana leaves turned over and twisted in the wind, the grass parted and flattened — pale green undersides were whipped horizontal. And there was that muffled announcement of a tropical storm, the distant weeping of rain on leaves. I looked up and saw it approaching, the gray skirt of the storm being drawn towards us. The Malays began running again with their corpse, but they had not gone thirty yards when the deluge was upon us, making a deafening crackle on the road and gulping in the nearby ditches.

The rice was planted. The rain continued.

It was about a month after this that we heard the news of the lawsuit. It was Peeraswami who explained it to me, and I am ashamed to say I didn't believe him. I needed the confirmation of Squibb and the others at the Club, but they didn't know half as much as my *peon*. For example, Peeraswami not only knew the details of the lawsuit but all that background as well — the arrangement that had been made in the *bomoh*'s hut and that tantalizing scrap of dialogue, "It is tiger's work."

What happened was this. After the death of little Aziza — after the first of the rain — the *kampong* held a meeting. Salim was wretched: the rain was proof of his daughter's curse. And yet it was decided that the remainder of the money would not be paid to the *bomoh*. Salim said that whoever paid it would be regarded as the murderer of Aziza — and that man would be killed; also, the *Penghulu*, the headman, pointed out that the fields were full, the rice was planted, and even if it did not rain for another six months it would be a good harvest. The *bomoh* had brought the rain, but he could not take it away. A Larut boy — in town selling butterflies to tourists — was given the message. There was no response from the *bomoh*. None was expected: it was unanswerable, the matter settled.

Then the *bomoh* acted. Astonishing! He was suing the *kampong*'s headman for nonpayment of the debt, a hundred and fifty Straits dollars plus costs. Peeraswami had the news before anyone. A day later the whole of Ayer Hitam knew.

"Apart from anything else," said Squibb, "they'll tear him apart as soon as they set eyes on him."

"He's a monster," said Angela.

"He must be joking," said Lloyd Strang, the government surveyor.

"If the *kampong* don't kill him, the court will," said Alec Stewart.

We consulted Stanley Chee.

"You don't know these Malay boys," he said. "They are very silly."

I had to ask him to repeat that. The rain made a clatter on the roof, like a shower of tin discs. Now we were always shouting, and the monsoon drains, four feet deep, were filled to the brim.

The *bomoh* was taken into protective custody and a magistrate was sent from Seremban to hear the case. The week of the trial no one worked. It was like Ramadhan: a sullenness came over the town, the streets were empty and held a damp still smell of desertion. Down by the jail a group of Malays sheltered under the eaves from the rain and called out abuse to the upper window.

I knew the court would be jammed, so the morning of the trial I drove in my official car with the CC plates and parked conspicuously by the front steps. A policeman opened the door and waving the crowd aside showed me in. I saw the *bomoh*, sitting at a side table with an Indian lawyer. At a table opposite were the gloomy Malays, the headman, Salim, some others, and their Chinese lawyer. Two fans were beating in the courtroom, and yet it was terribly hot; the windows were shut to keep the rain out, sealing the sodden heat in.

The *bomoh* took his spectacles off and polished them in his shirt-tail. He had looked like a petty clerk; now he looked only frail, with close-set eyes and a narrow head. He replaced his glasses and laid his skinny arms on the table. The Indian lawyer, whose suit was stained with dark patches of sweat, leaned over and whispered to him. The *bomoh* nodded.

"The court will now rise."

The magistrate entered, a Chinese man in a black robe and ragged wig. He sat — dropped behind the tall bench until only his head showed — and fussed with papers. He called upon the *bomoh*'s lawyer to present the case, which, flourishing a truncheon of rolled foolscap, the Indian did. "My client is owed the sum — "

The headman was called. The Chinese lawyer squawked something about "blood money" and was silenced by the magistrate. Twenty minutes of wrangling, then the magistrate said, "I have heard both sides of this unusual case. I order that *Penghulu* Ismail pay within thirty days the sum of one hundred and fifty — "

There were shouts, screams, stampings, and a woman's wail briefly drowned the rain.

"Silence or I'll clear the court!"

The magistrate continued with his verdict. So it was settled. The *kampong* had to pay the debt and the court costs. When the magistrate had finished, the clerk of the court stood and shouted above the hubbub, "The court will now adjourn."

"What happens now?" I said.

A fat Tamil in a light seersucker suit next to me said, "They are going to try the blighter for murder."

I was afraid that if I left the court I'd lose my seat, so I stayed and talked to this Indian. He had come all the way from Singapore. He was a lawyer there in a firm that handled mostly shipping cases — "but I'm on the criminal side myself." This was a celebrated case: he knew the *bomoh's* lawyer and he explained the defense.

"Well, it's a fine point. A British court would have thrown the book at him, but these Malay chaps are trying to do things their own way." He grinned, displaying a set of rusted betel-stained teeth. "Justice must be seen to be done. It's not so simple with these witch doctors. They're always giving trouble. Traditional law — it's a big field — they're going into it in K.L. In a nutshell, this silly blighter *bomoh* is claiming he did not do the murder. Yes, there *was* a murder, but a tiger did it. You see?"

"But he won the other case — he got his money. So he must be guilty."

"Not necessarily. Contract was made with him. Breach was proven — you heard it."

"Which means he killed the girl."

"No, tiger killed girl."

"But he's the tiger."

"No, he is man. Tiger is tiger."

"I don't get it," I said.

The Indian sighed. "Man cannot be tiger. If tiger killed girl, tiger must be brought to trial. If tiger cannot be found, man must be released."

I said sharply, "It's the same damned person!"

"Listen, my friend. I will explain you for the last time. Tiger killed girl and *perhaps* man became tiger. *But,* if such is the case, he was not man when he killed girl and *therefore* man cannot be held responsible for crime. He can change shape, into monkey or tiger or what not. He can work magic. So traditional law applies."

"Has he got a chance?"

"No, but it will be interesting all the same."

The magistrate returned. The *bomoh*'s lawyer outlined the facts of the case, arguing along the lines the Indian next to me had suggested, and he concluded, "I submit, m'lud, that my client is innocent of this deed. He has never been to the *kampong* in question, he has never seen the girl."

The *bomoh* was put in the witness box and cross-examined through a translator. He sat with his head slightly bowed, answering softly in Malay. The prosecuting lawyer charged him, flung his arms about, rounded on him with accusations. But the *bomoh* said, "Yes, I took the money — half of it — but I did not kill the girl. A tiger did that."

"I am putting it to you that you are the tiger," said the furious lawyer.

The *bomoh* spoke, then smiled. It was translated. "I think that someone like you who has been to a school can tell the difference between a tiger and a man."

There was little more. An adjournment, the sound of rain,

the suffocating heat. Then the verdict: guilty. The magistrate specified the punishment: the *bomoh* Noor was to be hanged.

People stood and howled and shook their fists, and I saw the *bomoh* being led away, a small foolish man in a faded shirt, handcuffed to two hurrying policemen.

It was difficult not to feel sorry for the deluded witch doctor who had sued the *kampong* for breach of contract and delivered himself into the hands of the police. He was a murderer, undoubtedly, but my sympathy for him increased when his appeal was turned down. The people at the Club, some of them, asked me if I could use my influence as a member of the diplomatic corps and get them into the hanging at the Central Jail.

There were some stories: Father Lefever from the Catholic mission had visited him, to hear his confession — what a confession *that* would have been! — but the *bomoh* sent him away; in another version of that story, the *bomoh* was baptized and converted to Catholicism. Food was brought to the *bomoh* by a group of Larut tribesmen, and it was said that attempts had been made to poison it.

The failure of his appeal met with general satisfaction. Squibb said, "I'd hang him myself if they gave me a chance. I've got the rope, too."

The night before the hanging I heard a cry, a low continual howl. I had just come back from the Club and was having a brandy alone on my upstairs verandah. I closed my eyes and listened very carefully. I had not imagined it: it had roused the village dogs, who replied with barks.

I gasped and had to put my glass down. For a moment I felt strangled — I couldn't breathe. My mind hollowed and in its emptiness was only the sound of crickets and a solitary gecko. I had never experienced such frightful seconds of termination. But it was the rain: I had become so accustomed to the regular sprinkle it was like a sound within me. Now there was no rain, and it was as if my heart had stopped.

The sun — the first for many weeks — woke me the following morning, and hearing excited voices from the road, I rose and instead of having breakfast, took the car into town. There was a great mob gathered at the Central Jail, mostly Malays. I parked the car and pushed to the center of the mob, where there were half a dozen policemen holding the crowd back. A police guard in a khaki uniform lay in the mud, his arms stretched out, one puttee undone and revealing not a leg but the bone of a leg. And his face had been removed: he wore a mask of dark meat.

Fifty feet away the jail door was open. The hasp of the lock dangled — it had obviously received a tremendous blow. The Malays' interest was all in the dead man, stinking in that bright dawn, but what interested me was not the twisted hasp or even the disorder that led to the cells, the smashed bench, the overturned chair, but rather the door itself, which was painted that Ministry of Works yellow. It had been raked very deeply with claws.

"*Tuan!*"

I turned. It was Peeraswami, all eyes and teeth, and he hissed at me, "*Matjan!*"

16. Coconut Gatherer

"WELCOME, welcome," said Sundrum, tightening his sarong and showing me to a chair. He had raised his voice; there were children playing under the window, shouting and thumping against the frail wall of the house.

"I'm surprised you get any work done, with that racket."

"Children," said Sundrum. "I love them. Their voices are music."

It was my first visit to Sundrum's. I had met him at Alec's Christmas party, where he'd talked about the snow he had always wanted to see. Sundrum had been introduced to me as a teacher. I discovered later that he was a writer as well, Ayer Hitam's only novelist. And I was moved by that description: the Chekhovian character stifling in an airless provincial town, comforted by his books, puffing his pipe, casting ironic glances at his neighbors and keeping his diary up to date.

"So you have this symphony every day?" The children were still at it, yelling and banging.

"How else could I work?" said Sundrum. He was half-Chinese, half-Indian and so looked Malay, with a potbelly and a grin. It was a Malaysian grin, the result of the heat, and it seemed cooked into his face. "Foreigners say this is a noisy country. I never notice it — perhaps it is because I am so busy."

"I'd be embarrassed to tell you how little I have to do."

"Writing is my life," he said. "I realized when I was in jail that life is short. I've had to make up for lost time."

"You don't seem the criminal type."

"I was imprisoned for my views. It was during the Emergency."

"You must have had strong views."

"I was held a month and then released."

"I see." A month's imprisonment: people got that for letting mosquitoes breed in their back yard. But I was angry with myself for ridiculing his jail sentence.

Sundrum said, "I didn't suffer. I listened to the birds. It is a matter of perspective. Perspective is everything, don't you agree?"

"Absolutely."

"People come here and write about Ayer Hitam. They are tourists — what do they know?" He threw open his arms and said, "But if you live here it's different! You have perspective. You don't hear children screaming — you hear the voices of the future. Music."

I was sorry I'd mentioned the children. Was he trying to rub it in?

"This is quite a library," I said, indicating the bookshelves, a rare sight in a Malaysian household. A pedestal held a dictionary, which was open in the middle.

"My books," said Sundrum. "But what do they matter? Life is so much more important than books. I write, but I know I am wasting my time. Do you know what I always wanted to be?"

"Tell me."

"A gatherer of coconuts," he said. "Not a farmer, but a laborer — one of these men who climbs the trees. Have you seen them? How they scramble up the vertical trunks? They cling to the tops of the trees and hack at the coconuts." He motioned with his hands, illustrating. "They defy gravity.

And they see more from the tops of those palm trees than anyone on the ground. I have spoken to those men. Do you know what they say? Every coconut is different."

"Is that so?"

"Every coconut is different!" He said it with surprising energy. "They are the true poets of this country. They have perspective. I must say I envy them."

Coconut gathering didn't seem much of an ambition. I had seen trained monkeys do it in Ayer Hitam. But Sundrum had spoken with enthusiasm, and I was almost persuaded. I thought: At last, a Malaysian who doesn't want a car, a passport, a radio, his airfare to New York. He was the first really happy man I had met in the country.

"I can't climb the coconut trees," he said. "So I do the next best thing. I write about it. You see?"

He raised his foot to the low wicker table and with his toe pushed a book towards me. The title in green was *The Coconut Gatherer*. He said, "This is my tree."

"I'd love to read it," I said.

"Take it with my compliments," he said. "It is about a boy who lives in a *kampong* like this. He is a sad boy, but one day he climbs a coconut tree and sees the town of Ayer Hitam. He leaves home, and the book is a record of his many unfortunate adventures in the town. He is bitterly disappointed. He loses his money. He is starving. He climbs a coconut tree in Ayer Hitam and sees his *kampong*. He goes home." Sundrum paused, then said, "I am that boy."

A Malay woman entered the room with a tray of food. She set the tray down on a table and withdrew, self-conscious as soon as her hands were empty.

"I hope you're hungry," said Sundrum.

"It looks good," I said.

He urged me to fill my plate. It was *nasi padang*, prawns, mutton chops, chicken, curried vegetables, and a heap of saffron rice; we finished with *gula malacca,* a kind of custard with coconut milk and sweet sauce. Sundrum ate greedily, wiping his hands on his sarong.

"I wish I had your cook," I said.

"I have no cook. I made this myself. That girl you saw — she is just the *amah.*"

"You're not married?"

"I will marry when my work is done," he said.

"You should open a restaurant."

"Cooking is a creative activity," he said. "I would rather cook than write. I would rather do almost anything than write. For me, enjoyment is going down to the *jelutong* tree where the old men gather, to listen to the stories of the old days. They are much wiser than I am."

I couldn't mock him; he spoke with feeling; I believed his humility to be genuine. And again I was ashamed, for what did I know of the town? I had never spoken to those old men. Indeed, my life seemed to be centered around the Club and the Consulate, the gossip of members, the complaints of Americans. Sundrum said he envied the coconut gatherers, but I envied Sundrum his peace of mind in this green clearing. It was an aspect of life that was so often overlooked, for there was contentment here, and just admitting that made me feel better, as if somehow Sundrum represented the soul of the people.

After lunch he took me around the *kampong* and introduced me. My Malay was no good then; I let him do all the talking and I barely understood what he was saying. I was impressed by the familiar way he greeted the old men and by their respectful attitude toward him. And I think that if I could have traded my life for his I would have done so, and changed into a sarong and spent the rest of my days there, swinging in a hammock and peeling prawns.

"Don't forget the book," he said, when I told him I had to

go. He rushed back to the house to get it, and he presented it in a formal, almost courtly way. "I hope you enjoy it."

"I'm sure I will."

"You were very kind to come out here," he said. "I know it is not very exciting, but it is important for you to see the whole of Malaysia, the great and the small."

"The pleasure is mine."

He took my hand and held it. "Friendship is more important than anything else. I tell my students that. If people only realized it, this would be a happier world."

I hurried away and almost hated myself when I remembered that I was hurrying to a cocktail party at Strang's. Now it was clear that Milly Strang wasn't coming back, and Strang was behaving like a widower. He needed cheering up; he would have taken my absence to mean moral disapproval.

That night, after the party, to recapture the mood of my visit to Sundrum's I took up *The Coconut Gatherer*. I read it in disbelief, for the story was mawkish, the prose appalling and artless, simply a sludge of wrongly punctuated paragraphs. It went on and on, a lesson on every page, and often the narrative broke down and limped into a sermon on the evils of society. The main character had no name; he was "Our Hero." I was surprised Sundrum had found a publisher until I looked at the imprint and saw that it was the work of our local Chinese printer, Wong Heck Mitt.

I soon forgot the book, but Sundrum himself I thought of often as a good man in a dull place. He was a happy soul, plump and brown in his little house, and I was glad for his very existence.

It was a year before I saw him again. The intervening time had a way of making Ayer Hitam seem a much bigger place, not the small island I knew it to be, but a vastness in which people could change or disappear.

I had expected to see him at Alec's Christmas party. He was not there, though the party was much the same as the first one. I arrived at Sundrum's house one day in early January, and he looked at me half in irritation, half in challenge, the kind of hasty recognition I had become accustomed to: he saw my race or nationality and there his glance ended. He didn't remember my name.

"I hope I'm not disturbing you," I said.

"Not at all. It's just that I've had so many visitors lately. And I've been on leave. Singapore. The *Straits Times* was doing a piece about me."

His tone was cold and self-regarding, but the room was as before — bizarrely so. The same arrangement of books, the open dictionary, *The Coconut Gatherer* on the low wicker table, and at the window the children's laughter.

Sundrum offered me Chinese tea and said, "Listen to them. Some people call that noise. I call it music."

"They seem pretty excited."

"They caught a python in the monsoon drain yesterday. That's what they're talking about. The whole *kampong* is excited. They've probably killed it already." He listened at the window, then said, "They have no idea what I do."

"How is your writing?"

"Writing is my life," he said. "I learned that in jail when I had no pencil or paper. But I make up for lost time."

I said, "It must have been the worst month of your life."

"Month?" His laugh was mocking and boastful. "It was closer to a year! I'll never forgive them for that. And I know who was behind it — the British. It was during the Emergency — they couldn't tell us apart. If you were so-called native you were guilty. You people have a lot to answer for."

"I'm not British," I said.

"You're white — what's the difference? The world belongs to you. Who are we? Illiterates, savages! What right do we have to publish our books — you own all the printeries. You're Prospero, I'm Caliban."

"Cut it out," I said. "I'm not an old fool and your mother isn't a witch."

"I'll tell you frankly," said Sundrum. "When the Japanese occupied Malaysia and killed the British we were astonished. We didn't hate the Japanese — we were impressed. Orientals just like us drove out these people we had always feared. That was the end; when we saw them fall so easily to the Japanese we knew we could do it."

"Really?" I said. "And what did you think when the Japanese surrendered?"

"I wept," he said. "I wept bitterly."

"You should write about that."

"I have, many times, but no one wants to hear the truth."

"I take it you're having some difficulty being published."

"Not at all," he said. "I've just finished a book. Here." He picked up *The Coconut Gatherer* and handed it to me. "Just off the presses. It's coming out soon."

I turned the pages to verify that it was the same book and not a sequel. It was the one I had read. I said, "But this isn't about the Japanese."

"It is about self-discovery," he said. "Do you know what I always wanted to be?"

"A coconut gatherer?"

He looked sharply at me, then said, "I'm not ashamed of it. I can't climb coconut trees, so I do the next best thing. I write about it."

I handled the book, not knowing what to say.

"Take that book," he said. "See for yourself if I'm not telling the truth."

It was too late to say that I had already read it, that he had given me a copy on my last visit. I said, "Thank you."

"I'm sorry I can't offer you anything but this tea. My cook

is ill. She is lying, of course — helping her husband with the rice harvest. I let her have her lie."

"This tea is fine."

"Drink up and I will show you the *kampong*," he said.

The old men were seated around the great tree; a year had not changed their features or their postures. Seeing Sundrum they got to their feet, as they had done the previous year, and they exchanged greetings. On my first visit my Malay had been shaky, but now I understood what Sundrum was saying. He did not tell the old men my name; he introduced me as someone who had come "from many miles away, crossing two oceans." "How long will he stay?" asked one old man. Sundrum said, "After we discuss some important matters he will go away." The men shook my hand and wished me a good journey.

"What a pity you don't understand this language," said Sundrum, as we walked back to the house. "It is music. Foreigners miss so much. But they still come and write about us. And their books are published and ours are not!"

"What were you talking about to those old men?" I asked.

"About the snake," he said, and walked a bit faster.

"The snake?" No snake had been mentioned.

"The python that was caught yesterday. It is going to be killed. They think it is a bad omen, perhaps it means we will have a poor harvest. I know what you think — a silly superstition! But I tell you I have known these omens to be correct."

I said, "Have you known them to be wrong?"

"To you, this must seem a poor *kampong*," said Sundrum. "But a great deal happens here. This is not Ayer Hitam. Every year is different here. I could live anywhere — a schoolmaster can name his price — but I choose to live here."

I looked again at the *kampong* and it was less than it had

seemed on my previous visit, smaller, dirtier, a bit woebegone, with more naked children, and somewhere a radio playing a shrill song. I wanted to leave at once.

"I have to go," I said.

"Europeans," he said. "Always in a hurry."

"I've got work to do."

"Look at those old men," he said, and turned and looked back at the *jelutong* tree. "They have the secret of life. They sit there. They don't hurry or worry. They are wiser than any of us."

"Yes." But I thought the opposite and saw them as only old and baffled and a bit foolish, chattering there under their tree year after year, meeting their friends at the mosque, facing the clock-tower to face Mecca, talking about the *haj* they would never take and going home when it got dark. Islanders.

Sundrum said, "When I was in jail I used to hear the birds singing outside my window and sometimes I dropped off to sleep and dreamed that I was back here on the *kampong*. It was a good dream."

"You're happy here."

"Why shouldn't I be?" he said. "I'm not like some people who write their books and then go to Singapore or K.L. to drink beer and run around with women. No, this is my life. I have my books, but what do they matter? Life is so much more important than books. I have no wish to live in Ayer Hitam."

Ayer Hitam could be seen from the top of a palm tree; for Sundrum it was a world away, a distance that could scarcely be put into words. A year before I had seen him as a solitary soulful man, who had found contentment. Now he seemed manic; another visitor might find him foolish or arrogant, but his arrogance was fear. He had that special blindness of the villager. How cruel that he had turned to writing, the one art that requires clear-sightedness.

I said, "You weren't at the Christmas party this year."

"I went last year."

"I know."

"Were you there? I didn't know the people well. I went to gather material. I've finished with Christmas parties, but I still need perspective — perspective is everything. From the ground, all coconuts look the same, but climb the tree and you will see that each one is different — a different shape, a different size, some ripe, some not. Some are rotten! That is the lesson of my novel."

We had reached his house. I said, "It's late."

"I promised you my book," he said. "Let me get it for you."

I heard him crossing the floor of his house, treading the worn planks. No, I thought: every coconut is the same. It takes time to decide that your first impression, however brutal, was correct.

There was no party that night. After dinner I sat down with *The Coconut Gatherer*. The book was identical to the one he had given me the previous year, the friendly flourish of his inscription on the flyleaf exactly as it was in the other copy. But I read it again, this time with pleasure. I admired his facility, the compactness of his imagery, the rough charm of his sermonizing. It was clumsy in parts: he had no gift for punctuation. But I could not fault him for these mechanical lapses, since beneath the husk and fiber of his imitative lyricism so much of what he described was recognizably true to me.

17. The Last Colonial

THE PLANTER GILLESPIE swore he'd never leave. Though he remained embattled — one of the last colonials — the changeover from rubber to palm oil continued on the larger estates. After eighteen months of it, I saw a time, not very far off, when I would gladly close the Consulate — or what was more likely, sell the remainder of my lease to the Arabs or the Japanese. Gillespie wanted me to dig my heels in and stay; he typified the older sort of expatriate, his attitude was a definition of that exile — home was defeat. Estate managers who went home caught cold, drove buses, and lived an *amah's* life, cooking and doing dishes.

And then, like deliverance, Gillespie was ambushed, killed on the road to Kluang. His *syce* was handed pamphlets and allowed to go free, so we knew it was political. But even that aspect did not shake the others at the Club; they said that sudden burst of gunfire on the lonely road was preferable to a slow death in Baltimore — Gillespie was an American — and they took the view that he was luckier than some who, hacked by *parangs*, had gone home maimed.

I had been told to expect it as the natural result of our collapse in Vietnam, more guerilla activity in Malaysia, a resurgence of revolutionary zeal. I was not surprised to hear of incidents in the northern states, where there were borders and concealing jungle. But here, in Ayer Hitam? It seemed unthinkable. And I couldn't imagine why anyone here would kill to make a political point or want to repeat the old cycle of taking power just to give another group its turn in purgatory. Yet it had started, and one of the pamphlets handed to Gillespie's *syce* was titled *Sejauh Mana Kita Bersabar? — How Long Must We Be Patient?* It could have been the complaint of any political group — of anyone who wanted power. But in the circumstances it was a threat. If this was patience I trembled to think what a loss of temper might mean.

Seeing that the recessional might be bloodier than I'd expected, I decided to stick my neck out and see the Sultan about it — not in my official capacity, but informally, to find out, before State Department representations were made, what steps were being taken to deal with terrorists. Unofficially, I had been told that the Malaysian government expected American military support. Though they had not been turned down, Flint in the Embassy in Kuala Lumpur had told me, "They're whistling in the dark, but if it makes things easier for you tell them we're thinking of giving them air cover."

The American position was: we'll help if the casualties are yours. I decided to hint this to the Sultan in the Oriental — or at least Malaysian — way. My opportunity came a few weeks after Gillespie's murder when talking with Azhari, the District Commissioner, at the ceremonial opening of a palm-oil estate, I asked if the Sultan was going to be there.

"He doesn't travel," said Azhari, as if the Sultan were some rare wine. He searched my face suspiciously: had I meant my question as criticism?

I said that I had been longing to meet him; that I might be leaving soon. "I'd hate to leave without having had a chat with him."

"I can arrange that," said Azhari.

I felt I had gone about it in the right way. The Sultan might get in touch with me, or Azhari might give me the go-ahead. I'd write a personal note and wouldn't mention security — I didn't want to talk to a general. But nothing happened. It was so often the case with the Oriental approach: one needed Oriental patience, like Gillespie.

It was a sign of our diminishing numbers, perhaps a siege mentality, that we began meeting together for lunch, Alec, Squibb, Evans, Strang, and sometimes Prosser. A club within the Club, for since I had arrived many expatriates had left and the membership committee started encouraging locals to join. It looked like tolerance; it was a way of paying the bills. Our lunches might have been a reaction to the Chinese tables, the Malay tables, the Indian tables. A multiracial club seemed to mean nothing more than a dining room filled with tables at which the various races asserted their difference by practicing exclusion.

At one of those lunches I noticed Alec carrying an odd familiar stick that I recognized and yet could not name.

"A shooting stick," he said when I asked. "You sit on it, like so." He opened it, stuck it into the dining room carpet and sat. There were some stares; the local members had not progressed to the point where they were allowed this sort of eccentricity.

"Going shooting?" asked Evans.

"Polo," said Alec. "I'm driving down to the Sultan's. This is the last day of the festival."

"Hari Raya Haji's months away," I said.

"Not that festival, you idiot. The Sultan's not a complete barbarian." He winked at me. "Polo festival. It's been going on for a week. This will be the best day — Pahang's playing. And tonight the Sultan awards his cup. But I shan't stay for that hoo-hah."

"Do you mind if I come along with you?"

Alec spoke to Squibb. "Hear that? I told you we'd make a gentleman out of this Yank."

And Alec even found me a shooting stick in one of the Club's storerooms. "Remember," he said, "pointed end in the ground. Got it?"

There were flags flying at the gateway of the Sultan's mansion, the flags of all the states, and colored pennants fluttering on wires. Across the driveway were the Christmas lights the Malays dragged out for special occasions. The day was overcast and sultry and the spectators looked subdued in the heat — a crowd of Malays standing on the opposite side, some still figures on our side, surrounded by many empty chairs. As we passed behind the awnings of the Royal Pavilion Alec said, "Just follow me and set your stick up. Don't turn around. Concentrate on the match."

"What's wrong?"

"He's here," said Alec. "I was hoping he wouldn't be. Worse luck."

"Who?"

"Buffles," said Alec.

"The Sultan?"

"Buffles. And if I catch you calling him 'Your Highness' I'll never give you lunch again."

We were not at the sidelines — Alec said we'd be trampled there. We had set up our sticks about thirty feet from the margin of the field, our backs to the pavilion.

It was to me an unexpectedly beautiful sport, graceful horses leaping back and forth on a field of English grass; like mock warfare, a tournament, chargers in the colors of chivalry, green and gold. No shouts, only the hoof beats, the occasional crack of sticks, and the small white ball flying from the scrimmage of snorting horses.

"Third chukka," said Alec. "There's Eddie Pahang — awfully good player. Get him!" Alec lurched with such excitement he drove his shooting stick deeper into the ground.

"I say, aren't you playing, Stewart?"

It was a high querulous voice. Alec sighed and said, "Buffles." But he turned smiling towards the striped awning. "Not today!"

I had not taken a good look at the Sultan when we entered the polo ground. Now I saw him and, seated next to him, Angela Miller in her garden-party outfit, white gloves and a long dress and a wide-brimmed hat. The Sultan wore a batik sports shirt and dark glasses; his head came to Angela's shoulder, her hat shielding him like an umbrella.

"Sit here, Stewart," he said, patting an armchair in front of him. "Join us — bring your friend."

Alec smiled rather coldly at Angela, as at a betrayer, then introduced me.

The Sultan said, "I didn't know there was still a consulate in Ayer Hitam. Why don't my people tell me anything?"

"It's really a small affair," I said.

"Ayer Hitam is lovely. Like those villages in the Cotswolds one sees. One drives through and always wishes one could stop. But one never does. Stewart, what do you think of the game?"

The Sultan was about seventy, with the posture and frown of an old toad. I had never seen a Malay who looked quite like him, certainly none as fat. And there was a greater difference — his skin was unmistakably freckled and in places blotchy, crushed, and oddly pigmented: strange for the ruler of such sleek unwrinkled people.

" — spirited," Alec was saying.

"Yes, spirited, spirited," said the Sultan. "That's just what I was telling Angela." He peered again at me, so that I could see my face in each of the lenses of his glasses. "Did you say you were a writer?"

"Consul," I said.

"But you know Beverley Nichols."

"I've heard of him."

"English," said the Sultan. "Frightfully clever. Wrote a book — " The Sultan fidgeted, trying to remember.

"The Sun in My Eyes, Your Highness," said Angela.

"That's it. Frightfully good book."

"His Highness appears in the book," said Angela.

"We must get it for the club library," I said.

"It's there," said Alec. "Nichols stopped for the night a few years ago. Gave us a signed copy. Bit of an old woman actually."

Angela said, "Literary gossip! It makes me homesick."

"He stayed with me a fortnight," said the Sultan. "I had a letter from him yesterday. His book was a best seller." He turned to Angela. "Someone's coming to stay. Lord — who is it?"

"Elsynge, Your Highness."

"Elsynge is coming, yes. Elsynge. Had a letter from him. Here," he said, "you two sit here. Do put those sticks away. You'll be more comfortable." He motioned to the armchairs in front of him and after we sat down he touched me on the shoulder. "Somerset Maugham — did you know him?"

"I never had the pleasure," I said.

"He visited," said the Sultan. "With his friend Earl, of course. Had to have Earl."

"He came to your coronation, Your Highness."

"Yes, he came to my coronation. He was here a week. But he stayed at Raffles Hotel. He liked Raffles. If he was alive to see it now he'd die!"

Alec said, "He's away!"

A pack of horses galloped down the field after one rider

who had broken away swinging his mallet. The handle curved as he hit the ball, which rose toward the goal. There was a great cheer from the Pahang side. The horses trotted away to regroup on the field.

The Sultan said, "Was that a goal?"

"No, Your Highness, but very nearly," said Angela.

"Very nearly, yes! I saw that, didn't I?"

"Missed by a foot," said Alec.

"Missed by a foot, yes!" said the Sultan and wiped his face.

"They're beautiful horses," I said. "I had no idea it was such a graceful sport."

The Sultan said, "Did you say you're a Canadian?"

"American."

"Do you know what a Canadian told me once? He said horsemeat is very good. This Canadian had pots of money — he owned all the cinemas in Canada. He went on safaris and shot grizzly bears in Russia and what not. He said to me, 'Bearmeat is the best, but the second best is horsemeat.' He said that. Yes, he did!"

Alec looked at me slyly and said, "That Canadian never tasted haggis."

"The *syces* here eat it," said the Sultan.

"Haggis?" said Alec.

But the Sultan hadn't heard. "My father was a sportsman. Oh, he was a great hunter. He shot everything, too, elephants, lions. He shot the last tiger in Malaya — the very last one! You might like to see his trophies after the match."

"We'll have to be heading back," said Alec.

"My father said horsemeat was good to eat. Yes, indeed. But it's very heating, he said." The Sultan placed his freckled hands on his belly and tugged. "You can't eat too much of it. It's too heating."

"You've tried it then?" I said.

He looked disapproving. "My *syces* eat it."

There was a shout from the Malays at the periphery of the field.

"What was that? A goal?"

"A foul, Your Highness," said Angela.

"A foul? What did he do?"

"Crossed over, Your Highness."

"Is that a foul?"

"Yes, Your Highness."

The Sultan grimaced in boredom. "Stewart, I was in Singapore yesterday. They gave me an escort and then they cleared Bukit Timah Road for me. Just closed the road. Too bad, chaps, they said. Took me fifteen minutes to get back from the Seaview."

"Fancy that," said Alec.

"The Bird Park's open," said the Sultan. "It's full of chickens, they say. Chickens of various kinds. They wanted me to see them. Know what I told them? I said, '*I* have *penguins.*' I do — eight or ten. Perhaps your friend would like to see them after the match."

"We're expected back in Ayer Hitam when the match is over," said Alec. He scowled at his watch. "Which should be any minute now."

"I won't let you go," said the Sultan. He spoke to Angela. "I won't let them go."

"No, Your Highness."

The match ended soon after she spoke. The Sultan said, "Come, Stewart," and he took Angela's arm. "If you don't come I shall never speak to you again."

Alec whispered, "He's not joking."

We were in the Sultan's ballroom. The lights of the chandeliers were on, and the fans rattled their glass. But it was not yet dark outside; the setting sun ridiculed these lights and made them look cheap, like the garish illuminations of an arcade. Some of the glass hangings were missing or broken; the wall mirrors were imperfect and had that tropical decay that showed as gray blistered smears on their undersides. I saw the Sultan's flowered shirt in one of the mirrors; it passed into a smear and he was gone.

The room was filled with people — women dressed like Angela, men in white suits, waiters carrying trays of drinks. The polo players were still in their uniforms, much grimier than they had looked on their horses, with mud-spattered boots. It was their celebration: they wore their mud proudly like a badge of combat.

"Have a drink," said a Malay polo player. He handed me a large gold cup.

The metal was warm and sticky, and I hesitated again when I saw the sloshing liquid, faintly yellow under a spittly froth. I tried to pass it back to him.

"Drink," he said. "It's champagne. We won!"

"Congratulations," I said, and made a show of drinking.

"It's solid gold," he said. "From Asprey's."

The cup was taken from me by a fat Malay girl who raised it to her mouth so quickly it splashed down her dress.

"That's okay," she said, and brushed at her dress. "It's just a cheap thing I got in London."

"Very pretty," I said.

"Do you like it? It's from a boutique. 'Che Guevara' on Carnaby Street."

"The Che Guevara boutique," I said. "That sums up the past fifteen years, doesn't it?"

She said, "The cup's from Asprey's. It cost three thousand dollars."

The polo player smiled. "Three thousand eight hundred." As he spoke his teeth snagged on his lip.

I was relieved to see Alec making his way toward us. He

greeted the girl, "How's my princess? You're looking fit."

"I'm not," she said. "It's this stinking climate. Daddy insists I spend my hols here. He knows I hate it, so he bought me a car this time. Red. Automatic transmission. It's the only one in the country."

"Drive up and see us some time," said Alec.

"You'd like that, wouldn't you?" she said. "Excuse me, I need a drink." She wandered into the crowd.

"The princess," said Alec. "She's a hard lass. Her tits are solid gold."

"Who are all these people?"

"Royalty of various kinds," said Alec. "They're all in the stud book. Try to look interested — we won't be here long."

"I was hoping to talk to the Sultan."

"I thought you'd had your fill of that."

"Political questions," I said. But I didn't want to ask them. I knew the answers, and I was certain it would only make me angrier to hear him say them.

Alec said, "It doesn't matter. Whatever you ask him, he'll turn the conversation to Beverley Nichols and Willie Maugham. Here he comes."

The Sultan entered the room. He had changed into a buff-colored military uniform that resembled a Masonic costume. None of the medals and ribbons thatched on his breast pocket were as stiking as the buttons down the front of his jacket, which turned the dim light from the chandeliers into a dazzle. There was some applause as he took his seat at the head table.

"Those buttons are something," I said.

"Diamonds," said Alec. "That's how we kept these jokers on our side, you know. We let them design their own uniforms. Buffles is one of the better ones. True, he barely speaks Malay, he's half gaga and he thinks Beverley Nichols is

Shakespeare. But I tell you, Buffles is one of the better ones."

"Isn't this rather an expensive farce?" I said. I looked around and thought: Gillespie died for them. But Gillespie had been a polo player.

"It's your farce from now on. You Americans will pay for it."

"No," I said. "They're whistling in the dark."

"We're being summoned," said Alec. "Here comes the princess. What did I tell you? Now we have to stay."

"No," I said. "I'm not hungry anymore."

The princess said, "Daddy wants you to sit down."

The Sultan had already begun eating. He was hunched biliously over his food and appeared to be spitting into his plate.

"We'll be right over," said Alec.

"I'm expected in Ayer Hitam," I said.

"Daddy said you're to stay."

"I'm afraid that's out of the question," I said.

Alec tried to soothe her, but she stepped in front of him and said crossly, "Daddy said so." She went back to the Sultan and whispered in his ear. The old man looked up, trying to focus on me. He looked blackly furious, and then his cheeks bulged with a bone which he spat on the table-cloth.

"Now you've done it," said Alec.

The princess returned to us. "Go, if you want to," she said. "Daddy doesn't care. But I do. You have no right to treat him that way. You know what I think of you? I think you're a typical rude American."

"If you believe that," I said, "then it won't surprise you if I tell you that I think you're a fat overprivileged little prig."

Her eyes widened at me. I thought she was going to scream, but all she said was, "I'm telling Daddy."

"Please do."

Alec said, "Are you off your head?" He rushed over to the Sultan and spoke to him, and he did not leave until he had the Sultan laughing, agreeing, sharing whatever story he had concocted to excuse himself for my bad manners.

"What were you telling the Sultan?" I asked on the way back to Ayer Hitam.

"Nothing," he said. Then suddenly, "You don't have to live here — I do."

The road was dark; we drove in silence for a while past the ruined rubber estates. At one, there was a shack at the roadside. I heard a child bawling. I said, "Poor Gillespie."

Alec grunted. He said, "Gillespie would have stayed."

He was right, of course. Gillespie would have stayed and charmed the Sultan and complimented the princess. I had overreacted — my squawk was ineffectual. But Gillespie didn't matter much. He was just another Maugham hero whose time was up. Only the night mattered, and those feebly lighted shacks, and the cry of that child in the darkness, and the danger that all of us deserved. We drove down the road which was made cavernous by hanging branches, and there was no sound but the pelting insects smashing against the windshield.

18. Triad

WE RATHER DISLIKED children; we had none of our own, but
that was seldom noticed because the local kids were everywhere. They strayed from the staff quarters and the *kampong*
into the club grounds, meeting in threes — three Tamils,
three Malays, three Chinese, as if that was the number required for play. They usually quarreled: it was an impossible
number — one was invariably made a leper, victimized, and
finally rejected. Alec called them villains. He blamed the
theft of his camera on one particular threesome who played
their own version — no teams, no net — of the Malay game
of *sepak takraw*, kicking a raffia ball the size of a grapefruit
back and forth at the side of the clubhouse.

There was a solitary one, perhaps Malay. It was hard to tell
how dark she was beneath her dirt. She had uncombed hair
and bruised legs and elbows and she wore a soiled waistless
dress of the sort sent in bales from America and England and
distributed by bush missionaries. She was not tall, but neither
was she very young. The dirt gave her skin the texture of
greasy fabric. Her feet were cracked like an adult's, she was
solemn, she did not play. She squatted on the grass with her
arms folded on her knees, her tangled hair drooping, and she
watched the other children taking possession of the parking
lot, the gardens, the old bowling green. She looked upon

them with a witchy aloofness. She was, for all her dirt, free.
All this I remembered after she joined us.

Late one night, over drinks, Tony Evans was describing
how a tennis ball should strike the racket if it was to have
maximum top-spin. There were three of us in the lounge —
Tony, Rupert Prosser, and myself — and it was October, just
before the second monsoon. Tony was still in his white tennis
outfit, having made a night of his after-game drinks; there
were spills of pink Angostura down the front of his Fred Perry
shirt.

"You should concentrate on your game now that the Footlighters have folded," he said to Prosser, the pink gins giving
what was meant as a casual remark a leaden pedantry. "Jan's
got a weak serve — she should be working on that." He
sipped his drink. "Now, top-spin. Ideally, the ball should hit
the racket at this angle."

He touched the ball to the strings and then with a sudden
hilarity hit the ball hard. It shot out of the window and made
a dark thump in the grass.

"You weren't paying attention."

Prosser said, "You're drunk."

But Evans was heading for the door. He said, "Now I've
got to find my bloody ball."

We heard him stamping around the lawn and swishing
through the flowers under the window. He cursed; there was
a cry — not his — like a cat's complaint. The next we knew
he was at the door and saying, "Look what I found!"

He did not hold the girl in his arms — she was too big for
that. He held her wrist, as if he was abducting her, and she
was trying to pull away. She had the haggard, insolent look of
someone startled from sleep. She did not seem afraid, but
rather contemptuous of us.

"She was at the door," said Evans. "I saw her legs sticking
out. These people can sleep anywhere."

"I've seen her around," said Prosser. "I thought she was from the *kampong*."

"Could use a bath," said Evans. He made a face, but still he held her wrist.

In Malay, I asked her what her name was. She scowled with fear and jerked her head to one side. Her thin starved face allowed her teeth and eyes to protrude, and she smelled of dust and damp grass. But she was undeniably pretty, in a wild sort of way, like a captive bird panting under its ragged feathers, wishing to break free of us.

"Call the police," said Evans. "She shouldn't be sleeping out there."

Then he said with unmistakable lechery, "She doesn't look like much, but believe me she's got a body under all those rags. I felt it! Give her a bath and you might be surprised by what you find. All she wants is a good scrub."

I said, "We ought to call the mission."

"They'll be asleep — it's nearly midnight," said Prosser. "I'll ring Jan. We can put her in the spare room."

Prosser went to the phone. Evans picked up the bowl of peanuts from the bottle-cluttered table. He showed her the peanuts and said, *"Makan?"*

At first she hesitated, then seeing that she was being encouraged she took a great handful and pushed it into her mouth. She turned away to chew and I could hear her hunger, the snappings and swallowings.

Evans nudged me. "Listen to him" — Prosser was drunkenly shouting into the phone in the next room — "I'll bet Jan thinks he's picked up some tart!"

A week later the girl was still with the Prossers.

"She's landed on her feet," said Evans. "Couple of bleeding hearts. They always wanted a kid."

"She's no kid," I said. "Has Prosser told the police? Her parents might be looking for her. Who knows, she might have had amnesia." Evans was shaking his head. "She might be a bit simple."

"Not according to Jan. They're thinking of taking her on as an *amah*. She learns fast, they say. The only thing is, she hasn't said a blessed word!"

"Suppose she's not Malay? Suppose she's Chinese? We should get someone to talk to her in Cantonese or Hokkien. Father Lefever could do it."

"You don't want a mish for this," said Evans. "My provisioner's just the man. I'll put him onto it. You're in for a treat. Pickwick's a real character."

That afternoon, as I was walking into town, a car drew up beside me, the Prossers' Zephyr.

"Give you a lift?" said Rupert.

I thanked him, but said I'd walk. Then I saw the girl. She was in the back seat, in a beautiful sarong, with a blouse so starched it was like stiff white paper enfolding her dark shoulders. She smiled at me shyly, as if ashamed to be seen this way. The blouse was crushed against her breasts, the sarong tightened on her curve of belly. Cleaned up she looked definitely Chinese; her face was a bit fuller, her eyes deep and lacking the dull shine her hunger had given them. She was a beauty in tremulous trapped repose, and the Prossers in the front seat were obviously very proud of her.

"We're taking Nina into town to buy some clothes," said Jan. "She doesn't have a stitch, poor thing."

"We had to burn her dress," said Rupert, grinning. "It stank!"

"Filthy! She was caked with it," said Jan, who like Rupert seemed to relish their transformation of the girl.

Rupert glanced back admiringly. "We gave her a good scrub. Jan wouldn't let me help."

Jan was coy. "She's hardly a child."

The girl hid her face against her shoulder: she knew she was being discussed.

I said, "What does she have to say?"

"Not much," said Jan. "Nothing actually. We think she'll open up when she gets used to us."

I told them my idea of asking someone to speak to her in Chinese and how Evans had suggested his provisioner.

"Wonderful," said Rupert. "Send him around. We're dying to find out about her."

"You know her name at least."

"Nina? That was Jan's idea. We always said if we had a girl we'd call her Nina."

And they drove away, like a couple who've rescued a stray cat. They looked happy, but I was struck by the sight of their three odd heads jogging in the car's rear window. If the girl had been younger, if she had not looked so changed by that hint of shame, I think I would have let the matter rest. There would have been little to describe: a lost child — and children look so much alike. But she was different, describable, almost remarkable in her looks, perhaps fifteen or sixteen, all her moles uncovered, a person. Someone would remember her. I knew Jan and Rupert wouldn't forgive me for going to the police, so the first chance I had I rang Father Lefever at the mission and asked him if he could find out anything about her. The mission net was wide: Johore was a parish.

Evans's provisioner was that unusual person in Malaysia, a fat man. I distrusted him the moment I saw him. He had an obscure tattoo on the back of his hand, three linked circles, and he had that wholly insincere jollity the Chinese affect when they are among strangers.

Evans introduced him as Pickwick and the fat man laughed

and said his name was Pei-Kway. He said, "Too hard for Europeans to say."

I stared at him, pursed my lips, and said crisply, "Pei-Kway."

Prosser was leading the girl into the room. She was even prettier than she had seemed in the car, but her look of wildness was gone; she was slow, uncertain, domesticated. She watched the floor.

"Ask her how old she is," said Jan.

"Go on, Picky, do your stuff," said Evans.

Pei-Kway spoke to the girl, and getting no reply he repeated his question in a slightly different tone, licking at the words and gulping as he spoke.

The girl's answer was little more than a sigh.

"Hokkien," said Pei-Kway. "She is sixteen years."

"Amazing," said Evans. "Small for her age."

"Not really," said Rupert. "Ask her where she's from."

This time the girl seemed reluctant to speak, and I could see that Pei-Kway was urging her. He was certainly challenging her, and he could have been uttering threats, his tone was so nasty. He did most of the talking, with greedy energy. The girl replied in monosyllables to his squawks. None of us interrupted; we stood by, lending Pei-Kway authority in what was by the minute becoming an inquisition. Though instead of going closer and bearing down on her, Pei-Kway inched back as he kept up this flow of questions.

He stopped. After all that talk all he said was, "She's not from Ayer Hitam."

"I could have told you that," said Evans.

"Doesn't she have parents?" asked Jan.

"Dead," said Pei-Kway. He made a vague gesture with his tattooed hand. He seemed satisfied, almost subdued. He had become as laconic as the girl; his grin was gone.

Now, unprompted, the girl spoke.

Pei-Kway said, "She wants to stay here. She is saying thank you." He said something to the girl in a harsh growl and I saw her react as if he'd given her a push.

I said, "What did you just say to her?"

Pei-Kway gave me a vast empty smile, simply a stiffening of his face. "I say, this is not your place." To Evans he said, "*Tuan,* I'm going."

But Jan had put her arm around the girl. "Wait a minute," she said. "Why is it she doesn't speak Malay? I thought everyone in this country knew Malay."

"They speak Hokkien in her village."

Rupert said, "Where is this village?"

"Batu Pahat," said Pei-Kway, who no longer looking at the girl was replying without referring to her. He appeared restless. He had announced his intention to go, but was kept at the door by the questions.

Jan said, "But what's her name?"

Angrily, Pei-Kway addressed the girl. Her mutter sounded familiar.

"Nina," said Pei-Kway.

For several days I saw nothing of the Prossers, but as usual when someone stayed away from the Club he became all the more present in conversation. Gossip and hearsay made absentees interesting and gave them a uniqueness that was dispelled only when they showed up.

Prosser's got his hands full," said Evans one day. "Nina tried to do a bunk last night. Found her sneaking out of the house. Scared rigid, she was. Had to carry her back bodily and lock her in her room."

"Lucky he caught her in time," I said.

"Very lucky, I'd say." Evans laughed loudly. "Imagine old

Prosser, who's in bed by midnight — and he sleeps like a bloody log — imagine him catching the girl leaving his house at four in the morning."

"You're sure of the time, are you?"

"Jan heard him. Maybe he was up splashing his boots, " said Evans. "But she's pretty, that girl."

I had not heard from Father Lefever. I rang him when Evans left, and he apologized for not getting in touch with me. He said he had found out nothing — he had completely forgotten about the girl.

"But now that you've reminded me," he said, "I will get down to business."

I told him to try Batu Pahat.

And yet I began to feel that I was prying. The Prossers seemed happy, and Evans's gossip I was sure was full of malicious envy. The girl had to be given a chance. If what Evans had said was true — that she had tried to get away — then it was only the fact of the odd numbers, the three of them. I pictured them in their bungalow on the oil-palm estate, playing at being a family, as the children in threes played their games on the Club's grounds. And I began to think they had succeeded with the girl in creating one of those outposts of intimacy so rare in the tropics, a happy family. They had left us.

There followed a period of dateless time, the hiatus of the delayed monsoon, hot and lacking any event; only the whine of the locusts, the occasional roar of a timber truck, the sound of the thin breeze rattling the palms, the accumulation of dust on the verandah that was more like sand or silt, bulking against my house. Silence and the meaningless chirp of birds, the scraw of lizards behind the pictures on the wall. I wished that I had, like Rupert Prosser, found a child in a garden at midnight that I could treat as my pet.

The mood was broken one afternoon by Prosser's voice saying, "Come over quick. I can't leave the house. Hurry, it's important. Evans is on his way."

"If anyone rings," I told Miss Leong, "I'm at the Prossers'. But I'm not expecting any calls."

Jan and Nina were on the sofa when I arrived. Nina was pale and held her face with the tips of her thin fingers; Jan was comforting her. Nina's face was shining with fear. Rupert was almost purple, and before I could speak he shouted, "They had her in a bag!"

Hearing this, Jan hugged the girl so tightly I thought she'd break. But the girl only drew her arms together, contracting in grief and closing her fingers to hide her face.

Evans's car drew up to the verandah. Rupert paused until he entered the room, then said again, "They had her in a bag!"

"Chinese?" said Evans.

"Three of them," said Rupert. "They must have been watching the house, because as soon as Jan left for her tennis they stepped in."

"Rupert found them — "

"I had an inkling something was wrong," said Rupert, and he swallowed hard, trying to resume. "I was at the estate stores and had this inkling. As soon as I saw their car I was on my guard, then three blokes came out of the house struggling with this bag. It shook me. I ran back to the car and got my pistol. They took one look at it and dropped the bag and drove off. They had *parangs*, but they're no match for a bullet. I thought it was a break-in — reckoned they had my hi-fi and Jan's jewelry in the bag. When I saw Nina crawling out you could have knocked me over with a feather."

Evans, with just the trace of a smile, said, "Lucky you came back when you did."

Rupert bent over and tugged his kneesocks straight.

"I didn't know you had a gun," I said.

"I was in Nigeria," he said. "I would have shot the bastards too, but they dropped the bag. I don't want any trouble with the police. You can get a jail sentence for shooting burglars in this bloody country. Burglars! But these were kidnappers."

"Probably political," said Evans.

"Sure," said Rupert. "Communists. They want to hold the estate to ransom."

"That sort of thing doesn't happen around here," I said. "This isn't Kedah. It might have been her relatives. Anyway, she's sixteen. You don't know much about her. She might be married. Her husband — "

Rupert said, "She's not married," and cleared his throat, "Dead scared, she was," and coughed, "I got their license number. But I don't want to go to the police because they'll start asking a lot of questions about who she is."

"The kidnappers might try again," said Evans.

"I'll shoot them next time," said Rupert hoarsely. "We'll move, get a transfer. But you've got to help me."

"I'd go to the police," I said.

"Don't you understand anything?" said Rupert. "We're keeping her."

Jan said, "We're determined now," and jumped as the telephone jangled.

"That'll be my wife," said Evans.

But it was Miss Leong. Father Lefever had called the Consulate. He wanted to see me immediately.

"I'm going over to the mission," I said to Rupert.

"I'll give you a lift," said Evans.

"I was hoping you'd stick around," said Rupert.

"You'll be all right," said Evans, giving Rupert a matey slap on the back.

In the car Evans said, "He thinks we're stupid. People come here from tin-pot places like Nigeria and they think they have all the answers."

"What are you talking about?"

"He discovered her trying to leave. He discovered some kidnappers. It's rubbish!" said Evans with greater outrage than I thought he was capable of. "He's knocking her off. He's setting the whole thing up. There was no kidnapping attempt. In a few weeks there'll be another disappearance, but this time it'll be the two of them doing a bunk, mark my words. Then you'll hear they're in North Borneo playing housie. Prosser's screwing her, the lucky sod."

At the mission I thanked him and started to get out of the car. He stopped me with his hand and said. "Who do you believe, him or me?"

"I believe the girl," I said, and saw that frightened face again.

Evans said, "She's not talking."

Across the courtyard, Father Lefever watched from his office doorway, and as I drew nearer I could see on his cassock — so white at a distance — grease marks and stains. A French Canadian, he had the grizzled appearance that dedicated missionaries acquire in the tropics; he usually needed a shave, his houseboy cut his hair. His sandals had been clumsily resewn, and yet these like the stains on his cassock seemed proof of his sanctity. Eager to talk he put his arm around me and hurried me inside.

"The girl," he said. "I think I know who she is."

I told him I had just seen her.

"Is she well?"

"She's rather upset."

"I didn't mean that. Is she in good health?"

"Father Lefever, someone tried to kidnap her today."

"Yes," he said, and shook his head. "I was also afraid of that."

"It was pretty serious. Three men came to Prosser's and put her in a sack. Prosser arrived just in time to stop them kidnapping her."

"He saved her life — they meant to kill her." Father Lefever fingered the knots on the rope that was tied around his waist. "It's the Triad," he said. "Probably the Sa Ji — they're the fellows who keep order around here."

Triad: the word was new to me. I told him so.

He said, "A Chinese secret society."

"Then it's not political," I said. "But Prosser doesn't have any money."

"Triads don't kidnap only for money," he said. He showed me the three knots on his rope belt. "It is like a religious order," he said, grasping one thick knot. "This obsesses them. Purity — but their kind of purity. And they punish impurity their own cruel way. A person is taken and put in a sack and drowned. They call it 'death by bath.' "

I saw Evans's point. He had guessed that Rupert had been to bed with her; and he had a good case — fortuitous finding of the girl about to escape, the visit home in the middle of the day: adulterer's luck. And now I understood Pei-Kway's tattoo.

"I suppose if the Triad thought she was Prosser's mistress they'd do that. Punishing the adultery."

"I didn't say anything about adultery," said Father Lefever. "They don't want her here, that's all."

"Batu Pahat's not far away."

"She doesn't live in Batu Pahat. Quite a bit off the road, in fact, at our mission hospital. I doubt that you've ever seen it. No one goes there willingly."

"A hospital?"

"A leprosarium," he said.

"She's a leper." I could not conceal my shock.

But Father Lefever was smiling. "You see your reaction? You're as bad as the Triad. It's not the girl, but her parents. Both have what we now call Hansen's disease. It's not so much a hospital as a village — very isolated, because people have such a horror of the disease. The girl probably doesn't have it, but what can she do? Her parents want her near them. She ran away six weeks ago. The priests were very reassured to know that she is safe here."

"What happens now?"

"You should tell your friends something of the girl's background. I'll put them in touch with the leprosarium and they can take it from there."

"They'll be horrified."

"Tell them not to worry. Even if she's a carrier it's only infectious if contact has been extensive. She's merely a houseguest — there's no problem."

Walking out to the courtyard, Father Lefever said, "They are doing great work at Batu Pahat. Why, do you know that two years ago your Mr. Leopold visited? He was much impressed. He's made a study of the disease."

"I don't know him," I said.

"Yes, you do. Leopold — he and his friend murdered that poor child in Chicago about fifty years ago. It was a celebrated case."

I delivered the news as tactfully as possible and withdrew, wondering what would happen. Though I had said nothing to Evans he knew all about it within a week — not from Prosser but from Pei-Kway. And Pei-Kway had the news that the girl had been sent back. I never found out what had gone on at the Prossers', among those three people; and the Triad was not charged with attempted murder. The only victim was that waif, who was made a leper, and each time I thought of her I saw her radiant, captive, in a new dress entering the leper village to join those two ruined people.

Jan stopped coming to the Club; Rupert was there every night until the bar closed. One weekend he went down to Batu Pahat. We didn't know whether he was seeing the girl or taking a cure, or both. He came back alone and seemed much happier; he talked of his great luck. Evans became fond of saying, "I give that marriage six months."

19. Diplomatic Relations

I IMAGINE that couples often forget they're married; I know that a person who is single remembers it every day, like a broken promise, that dwindling inheritance he is neglecting to spend. The married ones remind him of his condition — children do, too. He feels called upon to apologize or explain. He resists saying that he has made a choice. Where is his act? Bachelorhood looks like selfish delay, and the words are loaded: bachelor means queer, spinster means hag.

The hotel elevator stopped at every floor, filling with witnesses who brought me back to myself, to Jill's note. She was planning to stop in Ayer Hitam on her way to Djakarta — would I mind if she stayed a few days? She had specified the dates, her time of arrival, the telephone number and contact address in Kuala Lumpur where she could be reached. The flat belonged to her friend who was, like Jill, a secretary: the Embassy's sorority sisters. She told me how many suitcases she had. She was methodical, decisive; she had typed the note neatly. Several weeks later she sent a postcard repeating the information. She wasn't pestering. It was secretarial work.

And the only indication I had of her present state of mind was the form in which she sent the messages. The letter came in a "Peanuts" envelope — a cartoon of Snoopy on the flap;

her neatly typed note was from a joke note-pad titled *Dumb Things I Gotta Do*. The postcard was of a square-rigger and she had mailed it from Miami. I guessed that she had taken the windjammer cruise advertised on the front.

We had met in Kampala during my first overseas tour. As she was the Ambassador's secretary and I was a junior political officer she knew a great deal more than I did about the running of the Embassy. She showed me how to work the shredder, she alerted me to important cables. The fact that I was seeing her caused a certain amount of talk, embassy gossip, more class snobbery than a concern for security. The way she reacted to it made me like her the more: she never referred to her boss except by calling him "the Ambassador," she was discreet, she did not betray the smallest confidence. It was as if she had taken vows, and though celibacy was not one of them, secrecy was. She was so tactful about other people, I knew she would be tactful when my name came up. On the weekends we went to the loud dirty African night-clubs and danced to Congolese bands. I had made love to her on nine occasions — I kept count as if preparing a defense for myself, because I was sure we were watched. Eight of the occasions were after these dances; the ninth was the night before she left the country on transfer — I remember her suitcase in the living room and the stack of tea-chests awaiting the embassy packers. I was left with the sense that we had been deliberately separated.

She was sent to Vietnam, a promotion of sorts since her salary was practically doubled with hardship pay. There she stayed, in Saigon, while I finished in Kampala and was re-assigned to Ayer Hitam. At first she had written to me often; the letters became fewer, and finally they stopped altogether. I thought I had heard the last of her, then the "Peanuts" envelope came, and the windjammer postcard, the news that she was being sent to Djakarta. Knowing that I was going to meet her again I felt a thrill and a slight ache, the mingled sense of freedom and obligation at seeing a former lover.

Ayer Hitam was a considerable detour for her. I was flattered by her willingness to put up with the inconvenience. I looked forward to her visit. But I did not answer her letter immediately. Instead, I tried to recall in as much detail as possible the times we had spent together, and almost unexpectedly I discovered the memories to be tender. We had been alone, private, complete, for the short time we'd known each other, and she had shown me by example how to manage such affairs.

But the mind is thorough: seeking the past it casts us images of the future. I saw Jill in Ayer Hitam being joshed at the Club by Alec and leered at by Squibb and hearing how Strang grew watercress in his gumboots. At City Bar and at the mission she would look for more and see nothing more. In the town and at my house, trying to praise, she would miss what it took a year of residence to see, as if your eyes had to become accustomed to the strong light to perceive that the place had features, that the club members' ghastly jollity was a defense against strangers, that the weather was not as harsh in November as it was in June, or the aspect of the town — its dust and junk — as unimportant as it seemed. I would not be able to prove that events had taken place in Ayer Hitam; where was the proof? The past in the tropics is just the green erasures of wild plants. Jill was a kind person, but even her kindness would not prevent her, on a short visit to the town, from seeing the place as a backwater.

I wrote saying that I would be in Singapore on the dates she mentioned. Perhaps we could meet there? The letter went to her contact address in K.L. She phoned me when she arrived in the capital, said she understood and that Singapore was perfect. She was planning to fly from there to Djakarta to start her new job.

"What about Raffles Hotel — romantic!"

"It's not what it was," I said. "I generally stay at one of the plastic ones, the Mandarin."

"You're the mandarin," she said. "I'll see you there, Thursday at three."

"Will I recognize you?"

She laughed. "Probably not. I'll be the fat blonde in the lobby."

Everyone in the elevator was staring at the lighted numbers. For part of the descent I was giving myself reasons why I should not sleep with Jill; for the rest, reasons why I should make an attempt; and then we were at the lobby. She had not been fat before, and her hair had been dark, but she was partly right — she had put on a few pounds and her hair was now streaked gray-blonde. She looked, when I saw her sitting by the fountain, like a woman waiting for her lover — not me, someone older, richer, whom she would describe as a snappy dresser, a riot, a real card. She was sensible enough to know that she looked her best in a light suit, with make-up. She was of the denim and tee-shirt generation, but in matters of dress State Department employees are twenty years behind the times. She had obviously just had her hair done, she wore beautiful shoes, and her jewelry — four bracelets on each wrist, a necklace, a brooch — gave her the appearance of being bigger than she was, and slightly vulgar. Jewelry represents in its glitter a kind of smug self-esteem, cold and protective, like queenly armor. She looked safe and unassailable wearing her jewels.

She saw me and sat forward to let me kiss her, and she

lingered a fraction as if posing a question with that pressure. Perfume — a familiar scent, but much more of it, so much that it clung to my mouth, and each time she moved she created drafts of it against my eyes.

We did not speak until we were in the bar and touching glasses. She said, "You haven't changed. I know I have — let's not mention it here. I'm out of my element. How do you manage to keep so thin?"

"Dysentery. I've got the worst cook in Malaysia."

"Be glad you don't have me — I can't cook to save my life! Hey, the gal I was staying with in K.L. said you've got just the prettiest little Consulate. And you must like it because she says you never set foot out of it."

"I do, but I don't tell anyone."

"I forgot you were so young!" I saw in her smile and that wink — as obvious as a shade being drawn — pure lust. She was counting on me.

She said, "Did I tell you I was robbed?"

"You didn't mention it, no."

"I thought I told you on the phone. I've told everyone else. It was at that gal's flat when I arrived. My bags were on the landing. She let me in and when I went out for my bags the small case was gone. It couldn't have been there more than two minutes. They think a child did it. They've had other incidents. Of course, they haven't found it."

She did not look in the least distressed. She had lost her bag but now she had a good story.

"Was there anything valuable in it?"

"My watch. One I had made in Bangkok when I was getting Saigon out of my system. It's not the money — it was specially made for me. Sentimental value."

"If it was custom-made it must have been worth something."

She faced me. "It cost two thousand dollars. It had a jade face, diamond chips, and a gold strap. That was two years ago. It's probably worth more now. But it's not the money."

"I'd be in mourning if I were you."

"You're lying," she said. Her tone was affectionate. "But thanks — it's a nice lie."

I said, "Maybe they'll find the thief."

"I can always buy another one. But it won't be the same."

"A watch," I said. "Worth two grand."

"More like three. But friends are much more important than things like that." She met my gaze. "Don't you think so?"

I wanted to say no. I felt slightly blackmailed by the sentiments her loss required of me. But I said, "Sure I do."

"I was looking forward to seeing you."

This all came so neatly that I suspected a trick; she had baited the trap with something pathetic to arouse my sympathy and make me pause. Then she'd pounce. And yet I felt a futile indebtedness. We had been lovers — we were no longer. There was no way I could repay her except by a show of that same love, and that was gone. I did not feel the smallest tug of lust, only a foolish reflex, as if I'd seen two youngsters kissing and had to turn away to spare them embarrassment, to save myself from judging them.

I said, "I've thought about you a lot. Those terrible nightclubs. What a dreadful place Uganda was. But I didn't notice. You had such a cozy apartment."

"You should have seen it with the lights on. A mess. But I had a nice one in Saigon. It was in the compound — they all were — but on the top floor, air-conditioned, a guest room. I bought one of those waterbeds. They're fun, even if you're alone."

"Waterbeds in Saigon," I said. "No wonder we lost the war."

She winced, and all her make-up exaggerated this pained face as it had exaggerated her smiling one. She said, "I hated to leave. Sometimes I think of the others, the local staff, those telex operators and code clerks we left behind, and I want to weep. You never came to Vietnam."

"I was offered a trip, a fact-finding tour. I knew the facts, so I refused."

"You could have seen me. I'd have shown you around. I was hoping you'd visit. When you didn't I knew you'd thought about it and decided not to — you'd made a choice."

I wondered if she was being gentle with me by describing this missed opportunity: if I had gone, if she had shown me around, if I had made a gesture then, things would be different now.

I said, "Maybe we'll both be posted to Hanoi when we open our embassy there. It won't be long."

Jill said, "They shoot dogs in Hanoi. They won't shoot my Alfie."

"You have a dog?"

"Upstairs. Wouldn't travel without him. A cocker spaniel."

"You didn't have a dog in Kampala."

"I inherited him in Saigon," she said. "He changed my life. I took him back to the States after the pull-out. I'm taking him to Djakarta."

"He's a well-traveled dog."

"You'd better believe it. In the States we crossed the country. We went all the way to Arizona together."

"I thought you were from Ohio."

"I bought some land in Arizona." She saw my interest and added, "Twenty acres."

This, like the expensive watch, baffled me. She had told me once how after her father had died she'd gone to secretarial school in Cleveland, because it was cheaper than college. She had worked for three years supporting her mother: the single person always has a significant parent, inevitably a burden. But her mother had died, and Jill had joined the Foreign Service, to leave Ohio.

She said, "It's outside Tucson — it's good land. When I left Saigon I had so much money! We had all that hardship pay, those bonuses — everyone made money in Vietnam except the GIs. I thought I'd invest it, so we looked around, Alfie and me, and we settled on Arizona. It's sunny, it's clean, I can go there when I retire. I'll sell the land off in lots. Actually, I was thinking I'd sell half and use the money to build some houses on the rest, then sell those houses and buy myself a really nice one."

It was an ingenious scheme, and at once it all fitted together, the watch, the dog, the vacations, the jewelry, the land. She had made a choice. Once, perhaps, she had needed me; no longer. I could not be her life — this was her life. And seeing how she was managing — that however much she might have needed me she had never counted on me — I felt tender towards her and slightly saddened by the complicated arrangements that are necessary when we can't depend on each other. What precautions had I taken?

This security of hers was, if not an aphrodisiac, an encouragement. I had had two drinks, but seeing how safe and contented she was made me happy. She was managing; she wouldn't make demands. She was like that fabulous mistress, the older woman, either divorced or happily married who, with free afternoons, finds a man she likes and sleeps with him because she is energetic and resourceful and likes his dark eyes and believes that as long as she is happy she is blameless.

Land in Arizona: it reassured me.

I said, "How do you like this hotel?"

"The drinks are too expensive down here," she said. "I've got a bottle in my room. Shall we economize?"

"Whatever you say."

"It's time I fed Alfie. He's probably tearing the room apart."

Her room was on the fifteenth floor, and from the window I could see the sprawling island, the tiny red-roofed houses and the high-rise horrors. The hotel in the underdeveloped country is like a view from a plane. You are passing overhead and you know that if those people down there had this view they would overthrow their government.

I looked out the window so as to avoid staring at the room. The dog had been sleeping on the unmade bed, and as we entered he had woken and bounded toward us, whimpering at Jill, barking at me.

"You're all excited, aren't you? Yes, you are!" Jill was scratching him affectionately. "He's very possessive. Look at him."

The dog was shaking with excitement and rage. I thought he might sink his teeth into me.

Jill said, "That's pure jealousy."

There were shoes on the bed. One dress lay over the back of a chair, another over a door to the closet. Three suitcases were open on the floor and it looked as if the dog had pulled the clothes out. Jill's short-wave radio was on the bedside table with a copy of *Arizona Highways* and a Doris Lessing paperback.

She saw me looking at the novel and said, "Airplane reading. I picked it up in London. That gal has problems."

"Don't most gals?"

She looked hurt. "Don't most people?"

She had seemed so cool in the bar. Up here, in this cluttered room, it was as if I was seeing the contents of her mind, all of it shaken out. And I had known the moment I saw the dog that I couldn't do anything here — certainly not make love. There was no room for me; she could not have all this and a lover — she had made her choice.

"Is your room like this?" she asked.

I nodded. One suitcase, my pipe, my drip-dry suit. The opposite of this, and yet I envied her the completeness of her mess and saw in it a recklessness I could never manage.

"I love these little refrigerators. They must be Japanese." She walked towards the squat thing and the rubber around the door made a sucking noise as she pulled it open. "Same again? Here's the tonic, here's the ice, and here's the anesthetic." She had brought an enormous bottle of gin from the bathroom. "This was supposed to be your present for letting me stay at your house. Five bucks at the duty-free shop in Bangkok."

"I'm sorry about that."

"No, no," she said. "This is fine, a real reunion — I'm out of my element." She made herself a drink and crawled on to the bed. I noticed she was still wearing her shoes. She sat with her legs crossed, stroking the dog. She had moved through the clutter without seeing it; this disorder was her order.

I touched her glass. "To your new job."

"Same job, new place," she said. "And here's to your new place."

"I'm leaving Ayer Hitam in two months," I said.

"That's what I mean."

"So you knew."

She said, "I saw a cable."

"Where am I going?"

She said, "I forget."

Was this why she had come? Because no matter what

happened it wouldn't last; we would be parted, as we had been in Kampala. She had known she was leaving there — how wrong I had been to think I was the cause of her transfer to Saigon. That was her element, diplomatic relations, the continual parting. She was stronger than I had guessed.

I said, "Well, it's not Djakarta."

"No."

"It's far."

"They told you."

"No," I said. "You did."

She laughed. "If I knew you," she said, "I think I'd really like you a lot."

"Maybe you should have come to Ayer Hitam."

"I'm glad I didn't," she said. "What if I had liked it? It might be nice — flowers, trees, friendly people. I guessed you had one of those big shady houses, very cool, with gleaming floors and everything put away and a little Chinese man making us drinks."

I said nothing: it was as she had described it.

"Then I wouldn't have wanted to go. I'd have been sad, crying all the way to Djakarta. You've never seen me cry. I'm scary."

"You're not sad now."

"No," she said. "This is the place for us. A hotel room. Our own bottle of gin. Glasses from the bathroom. Couldn't be better."

I must have agreed rather half-heartedly — I was still thinking of her calculation in seeking me out just before I was to be transferred — because the next thing I heard her say was, "I suppose I should be sightseeing. Sniffing around. Every country has its own cigarette smell. Funny, isn't it? You know where you are when someone lights up."

I said, "I could take you sightseeing. There's only the Tiger Balm Gardens, a few noodle stalls, and the harbor."

"I'd hate you to do that," she said. "Anyway, this is a business trip for you. I don't want to be in your way." She winked as she had before. "Diplomatic relations."

As I raised my glass to her the dog growled.

"You don't think it's tacky, retiring to Arizona?"

"You're not retiring yet."

"So you do think it's tacky. But you're right — there'll be lots of assignments between now and then."

"Hanoi."

She said, "I'll hide Alfie in the pouch. I'll be your secretary. I'm out of my element here, but I'm a damned good secretary."

"Perfect."

She said, "It's a date. Can I freshen your drink?"

How appropriate those phrases were to her fifties chic, the girdle, the beautiful shoes, the lipstick, the jewels.

"Business," I said, and put my empty glass down out of her reach. "I have an appointment. You understand."

She did: I had reminded her that she was a secretary. She said, "Maybe I'll see you at breakfast."

"I'll be on the road before seven."

"Whatever you do, don't call me at seven!" She smiled and said, "Hanoi, then."

She knew she was absurd and insincere; she had no idea how brave I thought she was. She stood between me and the barking dog and let me kiss her cheek.

"Diplomatic relations," she said. "Off you go."

I went to my room and drew the curtains, cutting off the aching late-afternoon sun. I lay on my bed and tried to sleep, but it was no good. I felt I had revealed more to Jill in my reticence than if I had been stark naked and drunk. This thought was like a bump in the mattress. I did not wait for morning. That night I checked out of the hotel, roused Abubaker and went home. And now I knew why I hadn't let her visit Ayer Hitam: I didn't want her to pity me.

20. Dear William

For the past week or so, I have been putting off writing my report to the State Department — three pages to sum up my two years in Ayer Hitam — and then, this morning, your letter came. A good letter — what interesting things happen to people your age! You're game, impatient, unsuspicious: it is the kind of innocence that guarantees romance. I'm not mocking you. The woman sounded fascinating. But I advise you to follow your instinct and not see her again. It is possible to know too much. A little mystery is often easier to bear than an unwelcome fact; leave the memory incomplete.

Forgive my presumption. I haven't done my report, and here I am lecturing you on romance. I do think you'll be all right. You had quite a scare in Ayer Hitam — your bout of dengué fever has become part of the town's folklore. Isn't it amazing? What happens after the ghostly episode in the tropical place — the haunting, the shock? Of course — the victim picks himself up and leaves, meets a woman on the plane, and has another experience, totally unrelated to the ghost. Stories have no beginning or end; they are continuous and ragged. But the sequel to the ghost story must be something romantic or ordinary or even banal. I have never believed that characters in fiction vanish after the last page is turned — they have other lives, not explicit or remarkable enough for fiction, and yet it would be sad to think they were irrecoverable.

You mention getting "culture shock" when you arrived home. I know the feeling. You certainly didn't have it in Ayer Hitam. I'm sure you'll be back here sooner or later, as a contract teacher or whatever. It's fairly easy to get to countries like this; it's very hard to leave, which is why all of us who don't belong must leave. We crave simple societies, but they're no good for us. Now I understand why these rubber planters stayed so long — overstayed their visit, wore out their welcome. We have no business here. Up to a point — if you're young enough or curious enough — you can grow here; but after that you must go, or be destroyed. Is it possible to put down roots here? I don't think so. The Chinese won't, the Tamils can't, the Malays pretend they have them already, but they don't. Countries like this are possessed on the one hand by their own strangling foliage, and on the other by outside interests — business, international pressures (as long as the country has something to sell or the money to buy). Between jungle and viability, there is nothing — just the hubbub of struggling mercenaries, native and expatriate, staking their futile claims.

You asked about Squibb and the others. The others are fine. Squibb is another story. It was he who said, "I came here for two weeks and I stayed for thirty-five years." I didn't say anything, but I thought: Those first two weeks must have been the only ones he spent in this country that mattered.

He is so strange. I found it impossible to read his past; I have no idea what will happen to him. He told me that he had been in the club dining room when I entered, my first day in Ayer Hitam. He took credit for recognizing me — he discovered me — and sometime later he gave me the lowdown on the other members. He told me about Angela Miller's breakdown and how Gillespie used to drive an old Rolls. He filled me in on the Club's history — the polo, the cricket, the outings they made to Fraser's Hill just after the war. "Your people are all over the place," he said. And they were, too — though now, apart from missionaries and teachers, there isn't an American between here and the Thai border. "Gillespie's an old-timer," he said. "Plays polo. An American who plays polo is compensating for something. I've got no time for him." And yet Gillespie's murder shook him.

"Bachelor," he said, when I told him I wasn't married. "But you're too young to be a *confirmed* bachelor. Singapore's the place for a dirty weekend, by the way. Evans goes down now and again. Strang used to go, when his wife was on leave. His wife's devoted to him — you won't get anywhere with her. The Prossers are about your age, but they're new, and dead keen on the drama group. The locals are thick as two planks, the Sultan's a bloody bore, the missionaries don't speak to me, Angela's a rat-bag, and Alec Stewart's an odd fish. Yes, he's an odd one, he is."

I looked at Squibb.

He said, "He likes the lash."

I must have made a face, but he went on talking. Already he had taken me over. He had put it this way: if the people didn't like him, they would not take to me; if he found them odd, so would I. He wanted me on his side.

I hesitated, hung fire, or whatever the word is. I made him understand that I'd see for myself. And all this time, in the way a person offers information in order to get a reaction, he was searching my face, listening hard. He wanted to know what I was up to. What were my weaknesses? Did I drink, whore around, do my job? And, of course, was I queer?

I'm afraid I disappointed him, and perhaps many others. Typically, the consul is a character: a drinker, a womanizer, reckless, embittered, a man with a past, an extravagant failure of some sort with a certain raffish charm. I wasn't a character. I didn't drink much. I was calm. I thought I might make an impression on him, but if I did — on him or the others — it was not because I was a bizarre character, but because I was pretty ordinary, in a place that saw little of the ordinary.

I tried to be moderate and dependable, for the fact is that colorful characters — almost unbearable in the flesh — are colorful only in retrospect. But Squibb was angling. He wanted me on his side, and he searched me for secrets. He saw nothing but my moment of revulsion when he told me about Alec: "He likes the lash." I listened attentively: the Club Bore, that first hour, strikes one as a great raconteur.

He was what some people call a reactionary; he was brutal and blind, his fun was beer. It had swollen his little body and made him grotesque, a fat red man who (the memory is more tolerable than the experience) sat in the Club at nine in the morning with a pint of Tiger and a can of mentholated Greshams, drinking and puffing. Smoke seemed to come out of his ears as he grumbled over the previous day's *Straits Times*.

I used to wonder why he stayed, when others had gone. Like many so-called reactionaries he had no politics, only opinions, pet hates, grudges, and a paradoxical loathing for bureaucracy and trust in authority. He wanted order but he objected to the way in which order was established and maintained. If he'd had power he would have been a dictator — it was true of several other expatriates in Ayer Hitam — but weak, he was only a bore.

He wanted my friendship. He shared his experience with me: don't wear an undershirt, take a shower in the morning when the pipes are cold, keep drinking water in an old gin bottle, have a curry once a week, don't drink brandy after you've eaten a durian. That kind of thing; and as for unresponsive people, "Beat them," he said, "just beat them with barbed wire until they do what you want."

It was so simple with Squibb — you punished people and they obeyed. He had a theory that most people were glad to be dominated: it was the tyrant's contempt. "They like to be kicked," he'd say, and his mouth would go square with satisfaction. "Like Alec."

You know some of this. Wasn't it odd that he didn't like anyone — not anyone? That should have told us something about him. And he had failed at being a person, so he tried to succeed at being a character — someone out of Maugham. What tedious eccentricity Maugham was responsible for! He made heroes of these time-servers; he glorified them by being selective and leaving out their essential flaws. He gave people like Squibb destructive models to emulate, and he encouraged expatriates to pity themselves. It is the essence of the romantic lie.

Fiction is so often fatal: it hallows some places and it makes them look like dreamland: New York, London, Paris — like the label of an expensive suit. For other places it is a curse. Ayer Hitam seemed tainted, and it was cursed with romance that was undetectable to anyone who was not sitting on the club verandah with a drink in his hand.

"He likes the lash," Squibb had said, about Alec, and he looked for my reaction.

I couldn't hide it. I was shocked. I made a face.

"The whip," he said, giving a little provisional chuckle of mockery. "His missus beats him. The *rotan*. Pain. Why else would he be here? He was cashiered from the Royal Navy for that."

I didn't believe it, and yet what Squibb had said frightened me: it was cruel, pitiful, lonely agony. I could almost picture

it. What if it was true? We lead lives that even the best
fiction can't begin to suggest. Angela: was she the person
who had a nervous breakdown, the queen of the Footlighters,
or the Sultan's mistress? She was all three and much more,
but no story could unify those three different lives; they were
not linked. The truth is too complicated for words: truth
is water.

Squibb was animated that day, revealing secrets, trying to
obligate me with his own rivalries. What more damaging fact
could one learn about a doctor than that he was engrossed by
pain and had another life as the victim in some strange sexual
game?

I had said, "What will you say about me?"

"Ever tried it — the lash?"

I closed my eyes.

He said, "Don't take it so hard," and he gave me a gloating,
rueful laugh.

It was a brief conversation; it initiated me, it disturbed me
deeply, and it affected everything that happened after that. I
was circumspect with Alec, and Squibb went his own way.
Because of what Squibb had said, I never got to know Alec
very well. If Alec had a secret it was better left with him.
And we got on fine because I never inquired further. He
must have thought I was rather distant with him, and there
were times — when he looked after you, for example — that I
thought he was unnecessarily hard, confusing pleasure with its
opposite and seeing pain as a cure, or at least a relief.

The person who appears to have no secret seems to be
hiding something; and yet there is a simpler explanation for
this apparent deception — there probably isn't any secret.
We tend to see mystery in emptiness, but I knew from Africa
that emptiness is more often just that: behind it is a greater
emptiness.

I didn't like Squibb well enough to look for more in him. I liked Alec too much to invade his privacy. For the most part they stayed on the fringes of my life in Ayer Hitam. I didn't depend on them. I never felt that I had been admitted to the society here, but I began to doubt that society of that kind — ambitious order — really existed.

Sometimes, after a session at the Club, Alec would say, "I've got to be off. My missus is waiting." And I would get a dull ache in my soul imagining that he was going back to his bungalow to be whipped. It made me wince. I didn't want to think about it. But the one fact that I had been told made me suspicious of everyone I met, and when I realized the sort of double life that people led — and had proof of it — I felt rather inadequate myself. What was my life? My job, my nationals, my files: hardly enough. I wasn't a character; it was the other people who mattered, not me. I've always been rather amused by novelists who write autobiographically: the credulous self-promotion, the limited vision, the display of style. Other people's lives are so much more interesting than one's own. I am an unrepentant eavesdropper and I find anonymity a consolation.

So I have had an interesting two years. And it looks even better — more full — now that it's nearly over: teeming with incident. Those were hours and days. I've already forgotten the months and months when nothing happened but the humdrum hell of the tropical world, the sun directly overhead and burning dustily down; steam and noise; the distant shouting that might have been some deaf man's radio, the fans blowing my papers to the floor and my sweaty hand losing its grip and slipping down the shaft of my ball-point pen. Who wouldn't reminisce about ghosts, and even miss them a little?

I never made a friend here. If I had I think I would have seen much less of this place. I am old enough now to see friendship as a constraint. Perhaps, as you say, we will meet again. But I'm rambling — I was telling you about Squibb. Is there more? Yes, if you stay long enough, "look on and make no sound," and if you're patient enough, truth — colorless, odorless, tasteless — comes trickling out. Because no one forgets what he has said more quickly than the liar.

"You'll have to have a party," said Squibb, when he heard I was being posted back to Washington. Need I say our numbers have been substantially reduced? For Squibb, a party these days is a way of excluding the locals — he doesn't count his Malay wife. Remember, I barely know the man.

The party at his house was his idea — drinks. I had never been to his place before. Strang, the Prossers, Evans (he's off to Australia at the end of the month), the Stewarts. Squibb had the good grace to invite Peeraswami, but the poor fellow didn't know which way to turn — he looked at the little sandwiches, the spring rolls, the *vol-au-vents*. "This is having meat in it, *Tuan?*" he whispered. The shapes threw him a bit. Instead of eating, he drank; and he started talking loudly about the merits of Indian toddy. Then: "What will happen to me when you go?" Perhaps I have made a friend. Poor Peeraswami.

Stewart made a speech: "Our American colleague" — that kind of thing. Jokes: "I approve of nudity — in the right places," "Keep that bottle up your end," "How can you be an expert in Asian affairs unless you've had one?" After this, several embarrassing minutes of Alec's personal history, begun — as such stories so often are — by Alec shouting, "And I'm not ashamed to say — "

Peeraswami took out his hanky and vomited noisily into it. Then he ran out of the room.

As guest of honor, I could not leave until the others made a move. Without realizing it, I was wandering from room to room. Squibb has a library! Military histories, bad novels, Wallace's *The Malay Archipelago,* blood and thunder, and the usual bird and flower books one finds in every expatriate household. And souvenirs: sabers, spears, a samurai sword, bows, arrows, hatchets, Dyak weapons, Chinese daggers, a jeweled kris, and a rack of blowpipes that might have been flutes.

Squibb followed me in and boasted about how he'd stolen this and paid fifty cents for that. I saw a similar assortment on the wall of an adjoining room.

"More treasures," I said, and went in.

Squibb cleared his throat behind me as I ran my eye along the wall: bamboo rods, *rotans,* flails, birches of various kinds, handcuffs. They were narrow, shiny, cruel-looking implements, some with red tassels and leather handles, all on hooks, very orderly, and yet not museum pieces, not gathering dust. They had the used scratched look of kitchenware and — but I might have been imagining it — a vicious smell.

How was I to know I was in his bedroom? The bed was not like any other I had ever seen — a four-poster, but one of those carved and painted affairs from Malacca, probably a hundred years old, like an opium platform or an altar. I stared at it a long time before I realized what it was.

I said, "Sorry," and saw the straps on each post.

"No," said Squibb.

If I had left the room just then I think it would have been more embarrassing for him. I waited for him to say something more.

He picked up a bamboo rod and flexed it, like a Dickensian schoolmaster starting a lesson. He tapped one of the bedposts with it. The headboard was inlaid with oblong carvings: hunting scenes, pretty bridges, and pagodas. He said, "It's a Chinese bridal bed," and whacked the post again.

Something else was wrong: no mosquito net. I was going to comment on that. I heard the hilarity of the party, so joyless two rooms away.

Squibb, puffing hard on a cigarette, started to cough. The whips on the wall, the flails, the rods, black and parallel on their hooks; the heavy blinds; the dish of sand with the burned ends of joss sticks. I had discovered the source of his old lie, but this was not a truth I wanted to know in detail. If he had said, "Forget it," I would have gladly forgotten; but he was defiant, he lingered by the bed almost tenderly.

He said, "And this is where we have our little games."

Straps, whips, stains: I didn't want to see.

He laughed, his old gloating and rueful laugh. Two years before he had prepared me; and I had been shocked, I'd failed the test. Now I didn't matter: I was leaving in a few weeks. We were strangers once more, and he might not even have remembered how he'd made this all Alec's secret.

He put the bamboo rod back on the wall and glanced around the room. He seemed wistful now. What could I say?

"It's time I went," I said. He nodded: he released me.

This was a week ago. Since then he has treated me with sly and distant familiarity. I know his secret; it is not one I wished to know, but it makes many things clear.

So much for Squibb. Are you sorry you asked? There is no scandal. Apparently, I was the only one who didn't know. The scandal is elsewhere — the language barrier once more: I'm accused of calling the Sultan's daughter a pig. Being a Muslim, she objects. Actually, I called her a prig. It's all I'll be remembered for here. But that's another story.

My bags are packed, my *ang pows* distributed. As soon as it became known that I was leaving I was treated as if I didn't exist: I was a ghost, but a rather ineffectual one. Once a person signals that he is leaving he ceases to matter: he's seen as disloyal; his membership has ended, conviviality dies. But Peeraswami is still attentive: he covets my briefcase. I think I'll give it to him if he promises to look after my casuarina tree. I've already recommended him for a promotion; I'll deal with the others later, in my own way.

Now I must write my report.